Lose Yourself

Hook Up *or* Break Up

Lose Yourself

KENDALL ADAMS

HarperTempest
An Imprint of HarperCollins*Publishers*
A PARACHUTE PRESS BOOK

HarperTempest is an imprint of HarperCollins Publishers.

Lose Yourself
Copyright © 2007 by Parachute Publishing, L.L.C.

Library of Congress Catalog Card Number: 2006926606
ISBN-10: 0-06-088565-3 — ISBN-13: 978-0-06-088565-6
❖
First HarperTempest edition, 2007

Lose Yourself

one

"So . . . what do you say we go celebrate?" Zach asked. He slipped his strong arms around my waist and pulled me to him. I could seriously swim in those gorgeous hazel eyes. We'd been together three years, and the eyes *always* got me.

We were going to celebrate my tennis victory. My boyfriend, Zach Miller, hadn't missed one of my tennis matches all spring. And I hadn't lost one. Today was no different. I was fresh off a win against Eden Chou of Lawrencetown High. She'd given me a hell of a fight, and there were a few moments where I thought she would come back and hand me my first loss of the season. But, thank God she didn't. I, Noelle Bairstow, was the only singles player left in our suburban-Chicago athletic division without a loss. I'm not saying there's any correlation, but one *could* theorize that Zach was my good-luck charm.

"What did you have in mind?" I teased. Flirting came easily with a boyfriend as hot as Zach. Today he looked incredibly cute in his distressed jeans, white T-shirt, and a Jefferson High baseball cap that covered his spiky brown hair. Six foot two, broad shoulders, that little bit of stubble along his jaw. Half the girls from the other school were staring.

"Ugh! Get a room!" my best friend Aurora protested. "Or at least a Porta-Potti," she said, gesturing at the metal cubicle near the court.

"Um, ew?" my other best friend Danielle said.

As always, Zach ignored Aurora. But with her ripped fishnets, heavily ringed fingers, and pink streaks in her short black hair, that was actually pretty hard to do. I'm sure she'd earned her fair share of disturbed glances from the adults at the match who were wondering why she was even there. Did she make a wrong turn on her way to a rave?

On the outside, Aurora Darling and I might look like polar opposites, but on the inside we're almost freakishly similar. We became friends on the first day of kindergarten when she carefully scrutinized the entire class and decided to offer me her extra RingPop. You gotta love a girl who deems you worthy of her extra RingPop. We've shared all our secrets and hopes—and, of course, candy—ever since.

Danielle Ruiz, on the other hand, fits the tennis-girl stereotype like me. She was still glowing from her own win, her long dark hair pulled back in its usual thick braid.

Danielle and I met on the first day of practice freshman year and had bonded instantly over our equal lust for competition. It took a little while for her and Aurora to get used to each other, but that summer *they* discovered a shared lust for *Napoleon Dynamite*, which I just did not understand. We'd been a threesome ever since, though their taste in movies continues to baffle me.

"Let's see . . . how do you celebrate with the most dominant tennis player in the greater Chicago area? I'll have to think a minute," he said.

"'Most dominant' is right," Danielle said. "I'm glad *I* don't have to play you. Who knew a scrawny-ass girl could have such power?"

I rolled my eyes as I shoved my racket into its case. My friends were always teasing me for being super-skinny. It was irritating sometimes, actually. I wasn't big into dieting or anything—my size was in my genes. High metabolism, small bones. Sometimes I got the vibe that they were jealous I didn't have to work at it, but what could I do? Besides, along with the skinniness came my awkwardly towering height, tiny boobs, and humongous feet. I also inherited my mother's limp, plain-old-brown hair and my dad's plain-old-brown eyes. I would have killed for Danielle's gorgeous thick hair or her curves. And Aurora had these insane blue eyes and a cute, tiny figure that I would have loved to spend just one day in.

"Yeah, we'll see how far this scrawny ass takes me," I answered. "Getting to the state competition isn't going to be easy."

There wasn't much I wanted more than to win states this year. Last season, as a junior, I made it all the way to the final match, only to be trampled.

"Please, Noelle," Aurora groaned. "That girl whose butt you just kicked looked like her life was flashing before her eyes. Maybe more than one of her lives."

"She's right, Noelle. That girl's attack was a lot like Melanie's," Zach said, pushing his hands into his pockets. "You're totally ready."

A rush of adrenaline shot through me at the mention of her name. Melanie Faison was a cocky girl from our rival school, Washington High—and the very one who trampled me last year at states. She was having a killer season again, and everyone knew we were going to meet up in the finals. "Since when do you know so much about Melanie's game?"

Zach shrugged. "Just, you know, want to be up on your competition. Not that she is any competition," he added.

"Okay, let's not talk about her anymore. I'd rather savor this victory right now," I said.

"How about pizza and a movie to celebrate?" Zach asked with a sideways grin.

"Pizza I can do, but no movie," I said, hoisting my backpack and tennis gear over my shoulder. "I have that history exam tomorrow, and I have to go over my notes."

"That's our little Noelle," Danielle said with faux pride. "What would we do if she stopped overachieving?"

"We'd stop looking so lazy," Aurora joked.

"Right," Danielle said. "Actually, that would be nice. Could you stop now, Noelle?"

"Ha-ha," I said dryly.

"Don't listen to them. I like my women powerful." Zach reached out and slipped my tennis bag's strap off my shoulder and onto his. "Pizza it is."

Sigh. Did I mention that I love him? I so do.

Two slices of pizza and an hour later, I was leaning back on the velvety couch in Zach's basement, paying zero attention to the television. Zach lay on top of me, one leg between mine, his fingertips touching my face as we kissed. He'd lost the baseball cap, so I ran my own fingers through his hair. Now *this* was a celebration.

I sighed and kissed him more deeply. Instantly Zach's hands slipped around my back and up my shirt, groping for the clasp on my bra.

Damn. Had to remember. Sighs of pleasure were just as good as waving him on to the next base. I sat up quickly, and Zach dropped back onto his butt, surprised. He'd already unhooked me.

"You're getting better at that," I said, reaching around to refasten the bra.

"What's the matter?" he asked, staring at my hands as if they had betrayed him.

"I can't. Not today," I said.

"But it's the perfect time," Zach said, shifting his weight as I swung my legs around and placed my feet on the floor. "My parents won't be home for another hour."

"I know. But I told you, I have to study for that test."

I slid my ponytail holder out, then smoothed my hair on one side to retie it. On the other side Zach gently pushed my hair back and peppered my neck with kisses.

"Come on, Noelle. Blow it off," he murmured. My skin tingled. He knew that this always got me. Neck kisses were my downfall. "We're seniors. It's spring semester. We're supposed to be having fun."

Slowly I let him ease me down again, my eyes closed. Everything inside me throbbed. And we hadn't been together—really together—in a while. It was never easy finding time when we were both free, both in the mood, and in a parentless, comfortable spot. Maybe I could just—

Zach's right hand went for my bra again.

"No."

I sat up, and this time Zach scooted to the far end of the couch. Instantly the mood went from seriously warm to icy.

"I'm sorry," I told him, tying my hair back again. "I want to stay. I really do. But I have to keep my grades up if I want to keep valedictorian."

"And that's important . . . why?" he asked.

"I thought you 'liked your women powerful,'" I answered with a hint of sarcasm.

"I only said that to get your friends off your back," he replied.

"Gee, thanks."

He took one of my hands. "Don't go."

I bit my lip. I was not going to get into this argument

with him. Not again. We went through it every spring. His football and wrestling seasons were over, and he had nothing to do, so all of a sudden I was supposed to be there whenever he wanted me to be. Never mind the fact that I had tennis and my job and my grades to keep up. Spring was always tense for us, but today I didn't feel like playing into it. I'd won my match, and I was in a good mood. I wasn't going to let him bring me down. He knew my grades were important to me, even if we were about to graduate. If he loved me, he should try to understand.

"I have to," I said. Then I leaned in, gave him a quick but firm kiss, and got up. "I'll call you later. I love you."

"Yeah. I love you, too," he grumbled.

He turned up the volume on the TV and sat back, not even looking up as I walked out.

"He can be such a baby!" I shouted so Ryan Corcoran could hear me over the hissing and spitting of the cappuccino machine on Saturday afternoon. "I mean, he was, like, *sulking!*"

"Sounds like a real winner!" Ryan shouted back.

"You always say that!"

"I always mean it!"

I shook my head as the machine finally finished doing its thing.

Ryan and I had been working together at the Magic Bean, a local, family-owned coffee shop, since the fall. Last year for my seventeenth birthday, my parents bought me a car on the condition that I hold down a part-time job to pay for the gas and any repairs. A big "responsibility lesson."

My first job had been as a counter girl for Dairy Queen, but I quit at the end of the summer after one too many stomachaches from eating Oreo Blizzards. Then I applied here. It was my mother's favorite coffee haunt, and I'd been coming with her since I was a kid. I felt right at home among the exposed brick walls, overstuffed chairs, cracked tile tables, and colorful modern art. Ryan, who was a freshman at the local state college, had been the shift manager on duty the day I applied, and he hired me after approximately four minutes of chatting about music and movies— all of which we agreed on. Probably the easiest interview I would ever have.

"What do your friends think about this attitude he's giving you?" Ryan asked, pouring out a steaming hot cappuccino for the middle-aged woman waiting by the register.

I leaned back against the counter and toyed with the strings on my orange apron. "They kind of don't know."

Ryan handed the customer some change, thanked her, and slammed the register drawer.

"Come again?" He wiped his hands on his apron and turned around with an incredulous look on his face. His unbelievably handsome, magazine-cover face. We're talking deep brown eyes, perfect skin, tiny stud in one ear, silver band around his thumb. Artsy, musically inclined, and beautiful.

It was *way* too bad he was gay.

"You don't talk to Aurora and Danielle about this stuff?" he asked.

"Not really."

"Why not?" he asked.

"Because . . . I don't know . . . everyone thinks Zach and I are this perfect match," I said. "We even won 'Class Couple,'" I said, throwing in some air quotes. "I just don't want them to know—"

"That everything isn't perfect?" he said, crossing his arms over his chest.

"I guess."

"But you can tell me," he said.

"Well, yeah."

Ryan smiled slowly. "Well, I'm honored." He placed a hand over his heart and gave a slight bow.

"So . . . what do you think I should do?" I asked, grabbing a rag and wiping down the counter.

"Uh, dump the thumb-head loser already?" he suggested.

I laughed and shook my head. Ryan always made me feel better, whether he was just joking around or giving me actual advice. As a guy, he had an insider's view I never could have gotten from Aurora or Danielle. He was so easy to talk to, and there was an added bonus of his not knowing my friends or other kids from school, other than to pour them coffee. There was zero chance anything I told him would get back to someone important. Not that he would have spilled. I trusted him implicitly. It was sort of strange: He was one of my best friends, even though I never saw him outside the Magic Bean.

"Oh! Hey! I almost forgot," he said. He grabbed his

battered leather bag out from a cabinet under the counter and pulled out a blue flyer. "Lazy Daze has another gig this weekend."

My heart instantly sank. Ryan had been inviting me to his band's shows all year, but I hadn't been able to attend a single one. As soon as I saw the date, I knew that this time would be no different.

"I can't come," I said with an apologetic grimace. "This Saturday is our three-year anniversary."

"You mean with the thumb-head loser?"

"Don't call him that," I pleaded.

Ryan snapped the flyer out of my hands and shrugged. "Whatever. There will always be another gig."

Crap. I'd hurt his feelings.

"I'm sorry," I said as he crushed the flyer back into the bag and shoved the whole thing under the counter again. "I swear I'll come to one this summer."

He straightened up and pushed his hands into the back pockets of his jeans. "No, really. It's fine," he said. "No big deal. I hope you guys have a good time. What're you doing?"

"I don't know," I admitted. "Zach's keeping it a secret. He always surprises me on our anniversary."

"That's nice," Ryan said with a tight smile. He was clearly still upset.

With almost perfect timing, Mitch Bookbinder stormed out of the break room. He'd gone back there to punch out half an hour earlier—so long ago that I'd forgotten.

"That's the last time I call that bitch!" he announced.

"What happened?" Ryan asked.

"Oh, nothing! I just got my heart broken by cell phone!" Mitch covered his face with his hands and let out a distressed cry. "By *cell phone*!"

Mitch was the only person I knew who could give Aurora's drama a run for its money.

"Excuse me for a second," Ryan said to me. He walked to the end of the counter, nudging Mitch with him, and they started talking in low tones. When I first started working at the Bean, there were rumors circulating that Mitch and Ryan were hooking up. They spent all kinds of time together and were always whispering or making plans, so it had seemed to make sense. But while Ryan and I often talked about my personal life, he never divulged the details of his own, so I never knew if they actually *were* together or if they were just friends.

But apparently they weren't together now, because Mitch was calling some other guy a bitch. I turned my back to give the two of them a little more privacy. Luckily, there was a distraction on tap for me.

"All right! I want a grande decaf mocha latte with extra foam, three shots of sugar, and a sprinkle of cinnamon! STAT!"

Aurora earned stares from everyone in the café as she traipsed in calling out her order. She was wearing green hair streaks today, along with a green T-shirt under a denim-and-leather jacket, and a pair of low-rise plaid pants. Danielle and Jonah Moss, Danielle's über-jock boyfriend—also known as Zach's best friend—trailed behind. The two of them were much more understated. Polo and cords for Danielle, denim and varsity jacket for Jonah.

"First of all, Kermit, this is not Starbucks. We have small, medium, and large," I said to Aurora, leaning into the counter. "Secondly, can you repeat that majorly complicated order?"

I glanced over her shoulder, expecting Zach to walk in next, but the door shut behind them.

"Great," Aurora said, putting her head into her hands. "Now I don't remember it."

"Whaddup, Noelle?" Jonah said, placing his hands flat on top of the glass pastry display and drumming with his palms. "Got anything good tonight?"

"There's this new cinnamon-and-raisin roll that everyone seems to like."

"Sweet! I'll take three," he said.

Boys and their appetites.

"Got it." I took out the tongs and started loading up a paper plate with the heavy rolls. "Where's Zach?" I asked.

"Weirdest thing," Danielle said. "He called Jonah and said he wasn't feeling well. Had to stay home."

My heart gave a little extra thump. That *was* weird. "Is he okay? He was fine earlier today."

Jonah lifted a shoulder. "Dude said he was booting it big-time."

"Nice, Jonah. Very subtle," Danielle muttered.

I handed over his cinnamon-raisin rolls.

Jonah took a huge bite out of one of the sweet pastries

and rolled his eyes back in ecstasy. "Oh. That's good stuff."

"Wow. It must be really serious," I said. "Zach wouldn't miss a Saturday night out if he was half dead."

"It's true. Remember last year when he had that awful flu and he went to Six Flags with us anyway?" Danielle said. "We'll take three coffees, regular. Here," she said to me, handing over her cell phone. "I know you want to call him."

"Thanks," I said.

Mitch walked by, waving on his way out the door. Apparently Ryan had calmed him down enough to drive.

"Hey, Ryan, could you hook my friends up with some coffees?" I asked. "I have to make a call."

"Sure thing." He paused and looked at me. "Everything all right?"

"Yeah. I'm fine. I'll be right back."

I walked around the corner to the private end of the counter and quickly dialed Zach's number. I hoped he wasn't too sick. Maybe I could swing by after work and bring him something. Soup or crackers or one of those movies starring The Rock.

The phone rang three times. Four. Finally, on the fifth ring, the line clicked.

"Hey! This is Zach! Call me on my cell. If you don't have my cell number, your loss."

I was so flabbergasted by the answering machine, I was silent for a good five seconds after the beep. Zach had his own line, and he always picked up.

"Uh . . . Zach, it's me," I said. "Danielle and everyone

are here, and they said you were sick, so . . . I just called to see if you were okay. Call me back."

I hung up and quickly dialed his cell. Maybe he was in bed and his phone was too far away, but his cell was always nearby. He even brought it into the bathroom with him. This was a guy who hated missing anything.

His voice mail picked up instantly. I groaned in frustration as I listened to the message.

"Zach, it's Noelle. Call me at the coffee shop as soon as you get this," I said.

I hung up and took a deep breath. For some reason my heart was pounding fast and shallow, and my palms had grown slippery. In all the years I'd known him, Zach had never not picked up at least one of his phones—unless he was playing in a game at the time. He even insisted on keeping his cell on vibrate at the movies and would take every call, getting up and walking out to the lobby whenever it went off. He couldn't handle the idea that his friends might be out doing something without him.

He must be really sick, I thought. Either that, or something was up. I couldn't help the little flicker of uneasiness that flared inside me. This was totally unlike him. Was it possible, even the slightest bit possible, that he was *playing* sick?

"How's he doing?" Danielle asked sympathetically when I returned.

"He didn't answer," I said.

"Huh?" Danielle said.

"Exactly."

"Maybe he was . . . you know," Aurora said, waving a hand in front of her. We stared at her quizzically. She shoved an index finger into her open mouth.

"Pleasant," Ryan joked, capping the last of their coffee cups.

"I'm sure he'll call you back," Danielle said, grabbing my index finger and shaking it. This was her patented comforting gesture. I'd seen several generations of her family use it—mother, grandmother, great-aunt. Somehow it always worked a little magic.

"Yeah, you're right," I said. I handed her her cell phone as another pack of kids from school walked in. "I'd better get back to work."

Soon I was beyond busy, and Danielle, Aurora, and Jonah slipped out with a wave. I served up a couple dozen lattes, at least ten cappuccinos, a few Earl Greys, and a ton of sugary sweets before I finally checked the clock again.

Two hours had passed, and still no Zach.

That same uneasy feeling swirled through my chest. Where was he? Mr. I'll Call You Right Back. Mr. I Wouldn't Miss a Party Even If I Were Dead. Where, exactly, *was* my boyfriend?

two

Sunday afternoon Aurora and I trailed after my mother in the Rolling Ridge Mall as she Tasmanian-deviled her way from one storefront to another, oohing and aahing over the window displays, in search of a prom dress for me.

"What about red? You look lovely in red," Mom said, pausing in front of BCBG. "Actually, *I* might try on this one. Your father and I have that gala at the hospital coming up," she said, starting through the doorway. She paused and looked back over her shoulder at us. "Come on, girls!"

Aurora stared at me. "Has your mother ever been tested for speed?" she whispered.

"Trust me. I've thought about it," I muttered, trudging into the store after her.

My mother had my slight build and she was fit and

toned from a healthy routine of aerobics and Pilates. During the day, when she wasn't working with one of her occupational therapy clients, she was either at the gym or at the mall. Working out and shopping were her first loves—after my dad, me, and my sister. Thanks to all that exercise, she was one big ball of boundless energy.

I tried to get enthused as my mother whipped through the racks of glittery, floaty dresses, but instead I slumped back against a wall just as I had in every other store. I was exhausted from a night of tossing and turning, and my stomach kept clenching. All I really wanted was to lie down and take a nap.

Zach had never called me back yesterday. I checked ten thousand times to make sure the ringer on my cell was on. Now here it was, sixteen hours after my first call to him, and nothing.

"Oh! What about this?" my mother said, pulling out a gorgeous aqua gown with a halter top and a skirt that hung in various lengths. "You would look beautiful in this."

"You totally would, Noelle," Aurora agreed. "We're talking red-carpet good."

"Can't you just see her and Zach on a red carpet one day?" my mother gushed. "They are such a gorgeous couple."

"Mom . . . " I said, rolling my eyes at Aurora.

"You really are, Noelle," Aurora said with mock seriousness. She thought my mom was a kick and loved to humor her because it only made her gush more. Meanwhile, my mother loved Aurora because of her dramatic flair.

Back when we were little, Aurora and my older sister, Faith (a girl who is very in touch with her inner actress), used to force me to put on skits with them. My mother would always sit through every last moment of the performances and award us with a standing ovation.

"See? Aurora agrees!" she said. "You and Zach could go to the prom in brown paper bags and it wouldn't make a difference."

"We're not gonna wear brown paper bags, Mom," I groaned.

My mother looked at me—really *looked* at me—for the first time in the last hour, and concern creased her pretty face. I stood up straight and tried to look alive.

"Noelle, are you okay?" she asked. She came over to me and touched a cool hand to my face. "You're very warm, and you look pale."

I cleared my throat. "I'm fine. It's just hot in here, isn't it?" I shot Aurora a glance.

"Yeah. Totally," Aurora said. She looked a bit worried as well. "Maybe we should hit the food court, Mrs. Bairstow. Refuel a little. I'm gonna be needing a caffeine fix soon anyway or you'll lose me."

"The food court sounds like a great idea," my mother said, replacing the dress on the rack.

"Actually, maybe we should just go home," I suggested.

"Noelle . . . " my mother began.

"No, I'm serious," I told her. "I wanted to wait for Faith anyway. We always went shopping for dresses together. It's not the same without her."

This was true. Faith and I had always had fun trying on gowns together for our various dances and it would be a great way to welcome her home from her first year at Northwestern next week. But I also played the Faith card because I knew it would work on my mother. She loved the idea of her two very different daughters bonding.

"You're right. It's not," my mother said with a proud smile. "I'm sorry I didn't think of that before." She wrapped an arm around me and gave me a quick kiss on one temple. "But I still think we should go eat."

"Okay," I said with a sigh.

Back out in the mall, my mother broke off again, her window-shopping addiction kicking in. I took a deep breath and tried to calm my fluttering stomach.

"Hey," Aurora said, stopping me with a hand to my arm. "Are you okay? You look like a zombie."

"Thanks, Overreactor Girl. I'm fine," I said, forcing a laugh. "Just a little tired." I grabbed her hand and summoned up what little energy I had to pull her toward the escalator. "Come on! I'm feeling a little Burger King-y," I lied.

"Aw, yeah. *Love* the King." Aurora laughed and ran ahead to slide down the handrail—something she'd been warned about by mall security at least five times. I stepped onto the escalator, reached into my pocket, and pulled out my cell to stare at the tiny message-less screen.

Ring. Ring, dammit!

But it didn't. And now I was facing a long lunch with my mother and Aurora watching me like a pair of earnest school psychologists. All I could do was hope that my nervous stomach would actually manage to keep something down.

When I got home, there was a message from Zach. He hadn't even *tried* my cell like he always did. And when I'd called *him* back I'd gotten his voice mail. Again. He was definitely avoiding me. It was totally obvious. I wanted to know why.

So on Monday morning I was determined to find out. I waited for Zach in front of his locker. The football that the cheerleaders had taped to it back in November was still there. No one would dare tear it down, even though all the other team members' had been trashed by Christmas break. That was Zach. Most athletic, best smile, totally untouchable.

Until today. Today was the day his girlfriend would stand up to him and demand answers. Today Zach Miller wasn't going to weasel his way out of something just because he was Zach Miller. I was going to find out what was going on.

If my nerves would let me.

I heard his voice and his laugh just seconds before he rounded the corner, parting from Jonah and a couple of the other guys. I stood up straight and shook my hair back, scrutinizing him for some evidence of a weekend's worth of vomiting. There was none. Same self-assured walk. Same rosy cheeks. Same carefree smile.

My own stomach turned. Where was the waxy skin?

The pale lips? The tired eyes? That was how *I* looked after I was sick.

"Hey!" Zach said, wrapping me up into a bear hug. He smelled, as always, of Tide and evergreen aftershave. "I missed you this weekend."

I kept my arms at my sides. "Really? Then why didn't you call me back?" I asked.

He looked at me uncertainly, obviously sensing the chill, then started in on his combination.

"I did call you back. Yesterday," he said.

"That's about a day later than usual." I would not let his calm demeanor derail me. Something was up. I could *feel* it. "Where were you on Saturday night?"

"I thought Jonah told you," he said. "I was basically on the floor of the bathroom. You know, praying to the porcelain god?" He popped his locker open and shoved a couple of books inside. "What's with the third degree?"

"No third degree," I said with a shrug. "It's just, I was worried about you, and since you *always* call *everyone* right back, I was wondering where you were."

Zach slammed his locker hard enough to make me jump.

"I just told you where I was," he said harshly. "What did you want me to do, dial you up mid-spew? Or are you calling me a liar now?"

"No! Of course not." Zach never raised his voice to me. Ever. Even when we were fighting, he would just talk in a loud, intense whisper. "Why are you yelling?" I asked.

He took a deep breath and blew it out, unclenching his

hands. "I'm sorry. I guess I'm just tired. I didn't sleep much this weekend. I was up every five seconds feeling nauseated."

"Oh." The guilt was starting to seep in.

"Look, I'm sorry, okay?" he said quietly. "It's not like I didn't want to talk to you. I have a feeling it would have made me feel much better."

He reached over and cupped my face with one hand, running his thumb down my cheek. I looked into those hazel eyes and realized what a jerk I'd been. Zach had spent the entire weekend throwing up, and instead of comforting him, I'd accused him of lying.

Stop acting paranoid, I thought. *This is Zach. The love of your life. The guy who has been there for you every day for the past three years.*

We had our first kisses together, lost our virginity together, said "I love you" for the first time to each other. He wouldn't lie to me. Especially about something as simple as this. Right?

"I'm sorry," I said. "I'm a little out of it. It was a long weekend."

"Yeah. For me, too," he said pointedly.

I smiled. "I'm glad you're feeling better."

"Thanks."

He leaned in and kissed me, and I felt some of my suspicions start to subside. Everything was going to be fine. Why had I let myself get so freaked out?

"So, you wanna talk about our anniversary?" he said, looping an arm around my shoulders as we started down the hall.

I reached up with my right hand and held his just above my chest. "Uh, yeah!" I said. "It's only my favorite subject."

"Good. Cuz I'm gonna be picking you up at the crack of dawn. You'd better be ready."

"*Real*-ly?" I said, happy and relieved to fall right into our playful banter. "Why the crack of dawn?"

"If I told you that, it would spoil the surprise," he replied. He paused in front of my homeroom and gave me a quick kiss on the nose. *Liars don't give their girlfriends cute kisses on the nose,* I thought. "And I have so many surprises for you, your head will spin."

"Can't wait. I love you," I told him.

"Love you, too," he said, hitting me with one last kiss. Then he turned and loped off down the hall, slapping hands with various jocks along the way. No reason for paranoia here. No guilt, no guile.

Clearly it had all been in my head. It had to be. Otherwise he was the liar of the century. And I was just along for the ride.

As promised, I was waiting by the door at 8:00 A.M. on Saturday for Zach to pick me up. All week long he had refused to tell me where we were going, so I decided to wear khaki pants and a polo and packed a bag with a little black dress and heels, just in case. Every time a car drove by, I peeked out the front window. Honestly, I was even more excited than I had been for our first date.

Behind me, my mother and father washed the dishes in

the kitchen. I'd eaten a full breakfast of eggs, toast, and fruit, but now I was regretting it. When I was excited, my stomach was almost as easily agitated as when I was tense.

Finally Zach's black Xterra pulled up in front of the house.

"He's here!" I shouted, grabbing my denim jacket.

"Have fun!" my father called, leaning backward from the sink so he could see me through the door to the foyer.

"Take pictures!" my mom added, rushing out to kiss my cheek.

"Bye, Mom and Dad!"

I stepped into the cool spring morning air and closed the door behind me. Zach grinned from the front seat of the car and held up a bouquet of pink roses. He never forgot.

"Hey, beautiful."

"Hey!" I ran around to the passenger side and hopped in, tossing my bag into the backseat. Zach pushed his reflecting sunglasses up on top of his head and gave me a nice, long kiss.

"Happy anniversary," he whispered.

"Happy anniversary," I replied.

He handed me the roses, and I held them to my face, taking a deep breath. Ah. This was what having a boyfriend was all about.

"Buckle up," he said. "We have a long drive ahead of us."

"We do? Where are we going?" I asked.

"Still not getting that out of me," he replied. "But I will say that it's a good thing you were actually able to take off a *whole* day."

I blinked and lowered the flowers into my lap. There was a definite dig there. About how I was always working, always practicing, always studying, always unavailable. After three years together we were not immune to guilting each other. But I told myself he was just teasing, and I refused to let it get to me. I *had* taken the whole day off for him, for us, and we were going to have fun.

"Well, I was *happy* to do it," I shot back. I reached for my seat belt and strapped myself in.

Zach winked at me and smiled. "Then let's do it."

He hit the gas and peeled out. I yelped and grabbed the strap over my head, laughing the whole way. I couldn't wait to see where we were headed.

three

I sat forward on the metal bench along with all the other spectators, my pulse beating in my throat. The stands were utterly silent. On the pristine clay court down below, two of the hottest up-and-coming pro tennis players were going at it, diving and jumping in an exchange of the sickest shots I had ever seen.

"This is insane! How long has this rally been going on?" I whispered to Zach.

"Long enough that one of them is going to collapse soon," he replied with a smile.

With each shot the crowd gasped in awe. We were so close, we could hear the squeaks of the players' sneakers, their grunts of exertion, the *thwap* of the ball against their racket strings.

Finally Emily Rondale, the girl in the near end of the court, popped the ball up off the rim of her racket in a high arc. The entire crowd held its breath as her opponent, Christy Steiner, wailed on the ball, smacking it into the ground right at Rondale's feet, where it ricocheted off the court.

"Set! Steiner!" the ref called.

With that the entire mini-stadium exhaled as one. I leaned into Zach's side. The sun warmed my face, and a light breeze ruffled the newly green leaves on the trees all around us. The view from the stands was unbelievable. Lush green fields and old-school brick buildings. Who knew the Notre Dame campus was so picturesque?

"Having fun?" Zach asked, slipping an arm around me.

"This is hands down the coolest thing you've ever done for me," I murmured blissfully. "How did you find out about it?"

"I've been scouring the tennis sites for months, looking for something in our neighborhood that, you know, wouldn't break the bank," he said. "I read that Notre Dame was hosting this tournament and that there were some good players on the roster, so . . . "

I looked up, resting my chin on his shoulder. "You are amazing. I think you're my favorite of all my boyfriends."

"You slay me," Zach said dryly. Then he smiled and kissed my forehead. "I'm glad you like it."

"You know what would make it even more perfect?" I said.

"Don't tell me. Cotton candy," Zach answered.

He had spotted the vendor with his cardboard tray of pink fluff at the exact same moment I had.

"You know me too well," I said.

"I'm on it." Zach kissed me quickly, then jogged off down the stairs toward the guy in the striped shirt.

I sighed happily as I watched him go. I couldn't believe he'd driven two hours just to take me to see a live pro tennis match. How many girls had boyfriends who would go that far out of their way for them? Sure, we had our tiffs, but so what? This was the stuff that really mattered—the thoughtfulness, the attentiveness. Maybe we *weren't* as perfect as everyone at school thought, but we were pretty damn close.

Down below, Zach helped a couple of little kids carry six cones of cotton candy back to their family. He looked up at me and waved. My heart flip-flopped just like it did back when we'd started going out as freshmen. So sweet. At times like these I wondered what I had done to deserve a guy like him.

"Here you go," Zach said happily, handing over a small strawberry ice cream cone with chocolate sprinkles.

We'd already eaten dinner at Joseph's, the swankiest Italian restaurant in suburban Chicago. Now we were hitting Häagen-Dazs, just down the strip mall from the Magic Bean, the third and, I supposed, final stop on this whirlwind "Cater to Noelle" day. Too bad I was still stuffed from the chicken piccata, mashed potatoes, and garlic bread.

Zach, of course, was having no such issues. In his other

fist he gripped a waffle cone overflowing with cookies-and-cream and fudge sauce on top. I knew he would inhale it in about thirty seconds.

"This was so sweet of you, Zach—doing all my favorite things," I said, walking to one of the standing tables near the window.

"It was fun," Zach said.

"But what about you? I mean, it's *our* anniversary. We should do something for you."

Zach licked a bit of chocolate off his lip. "I just want to be with you," he said. "Doesn't matter what we're doing."

I flushed. Every once in a while he said the exact perfect thing. I leaned over and kissed his cheek. When I pulled back again, I was looking directly into Ryan Corcoran's beautiful brown eyes.

Wha-huh?

Ryan, who was standing outside on the sidewalk, seemed as startled to see me as I was to see him. But then he waved and headed inside. I placed my nearly untouched cone in the plastic holder on the table.

"Hey!" I said with a smile as the bell above the door tinkled.

Zach looked over one shoulder to see who I was greeting. When he saw Ryan, he went sort of stiff.

"How's the big anniversary celebration?" Ryan asked.

"Good," I said. "Winding down."

Ryan's eyes lit up. "That's perfect. I'm heading over to campus for that show I told you about. You guys should come."

"That's a great idea!"

"I don't think so."

Zach and I had spoken at the exact same time with the exact opposite sentiment. For a long moment none of us moved.

Then Zach took a deep breath and turned to me. "Noelle, this is *our* night," he said. "Don't you think we should be spending it alone together?"

I blinked. How was going to see live music not being alone together? There had been other people at the tennis match, at the restaurant, even here in Häagen-Dazs.

"We can just go for a little while. I've been telling Ryan all year that I would catch one of his gigs. It could be fun. And, hey, spontaneous! You're always telling me I should be more spontaneous."

Ryan exhaled noisily, and Zach and I both looked at him.

"Come on, Noelle," Zach said softly, taking my hand under the table. "It's our *anniversary*."

My breath caught at the sincere tone of his voice. Like he said, he just wanted to be with me. I tried to see it from his point of view. How would I feel if some girl I barely knew came in here and asked us to switch our plans for her?

Answer? Not good.

"Dude. It's just for an hour," Ryan said suddenly.

"*Dude*. Why don't you back off? I'm trying to have a private conversation with my girlfriend," Zach said, glaring at him.

"Guys. Calm down," I said, raising my hands. "Ryan, I'm sorry. Zach's right. We'll have to do it another time."

Ryan was clearly disappointed, but he nodded and shot me a quick smile. "That's cool. I guess I'll see you at work?"

"Definitely."

Ryan looked at Zach as he turned toward the exit. The derision in his eyes was obvious and intense. Zach glared right back at him.

"That guy so wants you," Zach scoffed after Ryan was out the door.

I burst out laughing. So *that* was it. He was jealous. And of Ryan of all people.

"What?" Zach asked, his brow creased. "It's as obvious as that humongous zit on his chin."

I hadn't noticed any zit. "Uh, Zach. You are *so* off."

"Uh, Noelle," Zach said, mimicking my tone. "I'm a guy. I can tell when another guy is after my girl."

"Well, you'd better adjust your radar, because that guy is gay," I said, taking a bite of ice cream.

"What?" Zach looked over his shoulder out the window as if he could still see Ryan. "Seriously?"

"Seriously," I said.

"Oh," Zach said. He dug a heaping spoonful of ice cream out of his waffle cone and shoved it into his mouth. "Good."

"Feeling better?" I asked, patting him on the shoulder.

"Much," he said with an ice-creamy smile. "Now let's get out of here."

"Where are we going?" I asked.

Zach shoved the door open so hard, it swung wide enough for me to trail through it behind him. "We have one more stop," he said. "The best one yet."

"Welcome to Hotel Miller," Zach said, opening the door from his garage to his basement for me. "Where romance is our mission."

I stepped inside, and my mouth dropped open unattractively. I could barely process what I was seeing. It was so over-the-top and so wrong, I had no idea what to say. Plus, it was clear from the giddy grin on Zach's face that he was expecting a completely different reaction than the one I was having.

"So? What do you think?"

"I think . . . "

What *did* I think? What did I think of the fact that he'd pulled out the sofa bed and made it up with red sheets? What did I think of the dozens of candles placed all around the room which he was now lighting? What did I think of the smooth R & B playing on the mini-stereo in the corner?

I felt as if I had just walked into some cheesy rent-by-the-hour motel.

"I wanted to re-create prom night, so I spent all yesterday afternoon shopping," Zach continued, clearly psyched. "I even went to the good Target."

I had to smile at that. I was always telling him how much better the Oakdale Target was than the one in town. Apparently he'd actually been listening.

"Zach, this is really nice, but—"

"What? Was it the Hotel Miller line? I thought that was stupid, but I wanted to—"

"It wasn't the Hotel Miller line," I told him. "But, Zach, what if your parents had come down here?"

"Please. They never come down here. I don't think they've come down here the entire time we've lived here," he said. "I think they're allergic to stairs."

He finished lighting the candles, walked over to me, and slipped my jacket off my shoulders. I felt a little chill and tried to turn it into a thrill of excitement, but it didn't play.

"Where are they now? Your parents?"

"They're asleep," Zach said, wrapping his arms around me. He started to step back and forth so that we were dancing. "That's why we came in through the garage."

"But they're here?" I asked.

"Yeah, but don't worry," Zach said, refusing to come down off his I'm-about-to-have-sex high. "They have no idea we're down here, and they're the heaviest sleepers on earth. Plus the door's locked. We can do whatever . . . we . . . want."

On each word he kissed my right hand, then my left, then my right again, as he backed toward the bed, tugging me with him.

"Remember prom night?" he asked, moving his hips against mine. "How we danced all alone in the room? And then we started kissing . . . "

I finally felt a little thrill then. Maybe I could get into this. Besides, he had done all this for me. He knew that having sex was a big deal to me and that I wished that every time could be as romantic as our first time, when he'd rented us a hotel room after the junior prom on his brother's credit card. We had talked about it for months beforehand and finally decided that we were ready, but we had still waited for the prom so that it would be perfect. Unfortunately that night had been *so* amazing and perfect for me that sneaking quickies on his basement couch since then had been kind of a letdown.

But he did this for you, Noelle, I thought. *All for you.*

"Yeah," I said finally, reaching up to circle his neck with my arms. "Yeah, I remember."

Zach smiled. He leaned in to kiss me and his fingertips trailed over my bare shoulders, sending tingles all over my body. He slowly untied the skinny dress strap around my neck, and I shivered—this time with a thrill of excitement.

Yes. I could get into this. No problem. No problem whatsoever.

four

"Omigod! Have you guys heard about Tracy Walkow's party?" Danielle asked, settling in at the end of our table in the cafeteria on Wednesday afternoon. "It's going to be out of control."

"Who hasn't?" I said, taking a sip of my apple juice. "I overheard this pack of freshmen in the hall this morning trying to coordinate their wardrobes. I think the entire school is going."

"Coordinate their wardrobes, like, to all wear the same thing, or to make sure they don't wear the same thing?" Aurora gestured with a carrot stick. "Because if it's to all wear the same thing, that is just sad."

"Actually, I don't know," I said.

"Well, what are you all gonna wear?" Jonah asked,

scooting his chair closer to Danielle and putting his arms around her. "Something sexy, I hope."

"Uh, we're not freshmen," Danielle said snarkily. "I don't know about you girls, but I don't need to be choosing my outfit four days in advance anymore."

"Especially not for some lame-ass party," Aurora said with a snort.

"Well, I won't be wearing anything," I said.

The guys looked at each other, perking up considerably.

"I don't know where this new Noelle came from, but I like her," Zach joked, smiling lasciviously.

"No! That's not what I meant." My face reddened. "I meant I don't have to think about what to wear because I can't go."

I took a bite of my grilled chicken sandwich but slowly stopped chewing as I realized everyone was staring at me. With some effort I swallowed the lump of food and winced as it scratched my throat. "What?"

"You're not going?" Danielle said. "Noelle, this is the first big party of the end of the year. Our *senior* year."

"I know, but the key word there is *first*," I said. "There will be others. And I have to work this Saturday."

"Unbelievable," Zach said, huffing through his nose.

I glanced at my friends. Everyone looked sort of skittish and uncertain. I saw Aurora and Danielle exchange a look, and my stomach churned. Was he really going to make a public scene? About *this*?

"Zach, you know I have to work two Saturdays a month," I said quietly. "And since I took last Saturday off—"

"Oh, so it's my fault, then," Zach interrupted. "I take you out for our anniversary, and now you're blaming me for your missing the biggest party of the year."

I pulled back and stared at him, stung. Tears burned behind my eyes. I couldn't believe he was picking a fight with me in front of all our friends—after everything we'd just celebrated.

"I wasn't blaming you for anything," I said. "I just have to work. That's all."

"Well, whatever." Zach pushed back from the table. "You can always join us later, you know, when you're done hanging out with your little coffee buddy."

"Are you talking about Ryan?" I asked.

Zach glanced around the group and for the first time seemed to realize how uncomfortable he was making everyone. Plus he'd basically just announced to the world that he was jealous of some other guy. "Forget it." He stood up, grabbed his backpack, and hovered for a split second. "I gotta go get my gym bag out of my car. I'll see you guys in class."

Then he turned and marched out of the cafeteria, every step stiffer than the last. For a long moment no one spoke. I placed my sandwich down on my plate and rubbed my quaking hands together in my lap. What was *wrong* with him?

"Whoa," Jonah said finally, shoving a few French fries into his mouth. "Trouble in paradise?"

He sounded so incredulous, it made my head hurt. As far as these people were concerned, Zach and I hadn't fought once in the three years we'd been together.

"Yeah. What's with the split personality?" Aurora asked.

"Noelle, are you okay?" Danielle said.

I forced a smile and blinked back embarrassed tears. "Yeah. I'm fine," I said. "I guess Zach just had one too many Red Bulls this morning or something."

"Dude cannot hold his caffeine," Jonah said, accepting this excuse immediately.

"You know what? I think I'm gonna go to the library and go over my notes for the French quiz," I said, getting up with my tray. "I'll see you later."

"Okay." Danielle still looked concerned.

"Want me to track him down and give him a wedgie for ya?" Aurora added.

I grinned. "That's okay. But thanks for the offer."

"Anytime."

I walked to the nearest garbage can, dumped ninety percent of my lunch into it, and headed for the door on shaky legs.

Saturday evening, I bent over the countertop at the Magic Bean, rested my chin in one palm, and stared at the empty chairs in front of me.

It was cold and windy, as if spring had decided to take the night off and let winter come out of retirement to take its shift. All the people who had been strolling the strip mall for the past few weekends, enjoying the fact that they could actually loiter outside, had decided to hibernate. The Magic Bean was like a tomb.

Which meant I had nothing to focus on other than the party I was missing. And the fact that Zach and I had barely spoken for three days.

The night of the cafeteria catastrophe Zach called to apologize and told me that he just wanted to spend time with me, which is why he'd gotten upset. In the fall I would be off to Princeton in New Jersey, and he would be back here at the University of Illinois. He said he just wanted to get in as much "Noelle time" as possible. It was all very sweet, and for a moment I had felt better. But when he realized I wasn't going to bail on my shift even after his speech, he'd gotten cold again. Which, of course, left me wondering if he'd only said those things to get his way.

I took a deep breath and let it out with a sigh. Sometimes being in a relationship was more work than fun. I tried to think about it from Zach's point of view. When it came down to it, my boyfriend was just upset because he wanted to spend time with me; he simply had a dumb way of showing it. And I wanted to spend time with him, too. Maybe I should have blown off work just this once. Last Saturday he'd gone to all that trouble to do things I wanted to do. It might have been nice of me to make a sacrifice for him as well.

A pang of guilt hit me hard in the chest. Was I an ungrateful girlfriend?

Suddenly a cardboard cup sleeve fell onto the counter right in front of me, startling me out of my stupor.

"Cup sleeve for your thoughts," Ryan said.

I stood up straight and got a head rush, so I leaned

back against the pastry case and closed my eyes for a second before answering.

"Whoa. You okay?" Ryan asked.

"Head rush," I said, trying to maintain my balance as I rubbed my forehead. "There's this huge party tonight, and I'm basically the only person from my school who's not there."

"I find that hard to believe," Ryan said. "There's gotta be someone else who's working. Or sick. Or, hey! There's a sci-fi convention in Chicago this weekend. You gotta have a couple of *Stargate* devotees at that school of yours."

I smiled sadly at his joke and looked down at the toes of my battered work sneakers. I wondered what Zach was doing right now. Probably standing in a corner, joking around with his buddies, being mad at me.

"Wow. You really want to be at this party," Ryan said.

"It's no big deal," I replied lamely, shrugging.

Ryan put his hands on my shoulders, startling me. I glanced up at him in confusion as he turned me around, grabbed the strings on my apron, and pulled. He yanked it over my head and balled it up.

"You're free!" he announced. "Run! Run like the wind!"

I laughed for real this time. "What?" I said, smoothing my hair as I turned around. "Come on. I can't leave."

Ryan opened his arms to take in the empty café. Empty except for one older guy who was pretty much always camped out in a corner with his laptop.

"Give me one good reason why not," he challenged.

"Uh, how about cuz you'd be here alone?" I said.

"So? I can close up by myself," Ryan stated. "Besides, it's not like you're going to be any help to me if you're catatonic."

I looked around at the deserted chairs and unused tables. There really wouldn't be that much work to do. But could I do this? Leave work early? It was so . . . spur of the moment. So irresponsible. So . . . not me. Slowly I smiled.

Maybe a not-me moment was exactly what I needed.

"Are you sure?" I asked.

"If you don't get out of here in the next thirty seconds, I *will* make you stay to clean out the cappuccino machine," he replied.

"All right! I'm gone!"

On impulse I leaned forward and gave Ryan a quick kiss on the cheek. The second I did it, I was embarrassed. It was a line that had never been crossed before. When I pulled back, Ryan was blushing, but I chose to ignore that. The last thing I wanted to do was make the moment more awkward by dwelling on it.

"Thanks," I said.

"No problem."

Then I grabbed my purse from the cabinet under the counter and ran to clock out. I couldn't wait to see the look on Zach's face!

The party was jamming. And *jammed*. Tracy had a pretty big three-story condo but not big enough to hold an entire school's worth of kids. The moment I walked through the doorway, I felt pressed in and claustrophobic. People milled around in every available corner, smoking, drinking from plastic cups, and shouting to be heard over the stereo. Why none of the neighbors had called the cops yet was beyond me.

"Excuse me!" I yelled at two large guys talking in the doorway between the foyer and the living room.

"Hey! Noelle Bairstow!" Derek Walton—senior, baseball player, and guy who had confessed his undying love for me during a drunken ramble at the Valentine's Day Ball after-party—was leaning against the door to the living room. He looked me up and down with his watery brown eyes and took a sip from his beer cup. Derek was one of those brave drunks: totally sweet and shy in school but bold and brazen when blasted.

"Hey, Derek!" I said, trying to slide past him.

He rested a heavy arm on one of my shoulders and loomed forward. "You look hot."

"No, I don't. I look like I just got off work," I told him. "Have you seen *Zach*?"

At the mention of my boyfriend Derek instantly backed off, so quickly that he bonked his head on the doorjamb. "Nope. Haven't. Later." And then he was gone.

I rolled my eyes and looked around. The couches were packed with at least twice the number of people they should have held. The TV was tuned to ESPN but on mute. Near a wall a few couples danced to the music, grinding and kissing and sloshing their drinks. There were several unfamiliar faces in the crowd. Apparently another school or two had heard about the bash.

"Noelle! Hey! You came!" Tracy Walkow shouted, appearing out of nowhere. She was drunk off her butt and fell into me as she tried to hug me. A bunch of people laughed as I stood her up and steadied her.

"Hi, Tracy!" I yelled into her ear. "Have you seen Zach?"

"Yeah!" she said, then hiccupped. "He's in the back-yard!"

"There are people outside? It's freezing!"

"I know! But the house isn't big enough," she said, taking another slug. "Whaddaya gonna do?" She threw her hands up, sloshing beer all over some poor guy's back, then almost fell over again.

"Are you okay?" I asked her.

"I think I'm gonna go lie down," she said. She wavered unsteadily and turned green right in front of me.

I looked around and spotted one of Tracy's good friends—a petite, hipster brunette named Donna. "Donna!" I shouted, waving her down. Donna took one look at Tracy and was over there in a flash. "I think she might need to go to the bathroom. . . . "

"Got it," Donna replied. "Thanks."

She wrapped an arm around Tracy and helped her toward the kitchen and the bathroom beyond.

Satisfied that Tracy was taken care of, I headed for the sliding glass doors at the back of the room. Several people were standing in front of and around them. When I shoved the door open, a cold blast of air hit me in the face, and everyone shouted.

"Hey! Close it!"

"What're you trying to do? Kill us?"

I mouthed a "sorry" and ducked out. There were a couple dozen brave souls in the backyard. On a chaise lounge a pair of lovers writhed and kissed, keeping each other warm. Three guys from the basketball team were playing drinking games at the edge of the patio. Lena Mardirossian pushed herself up from a chair and teetered toward me, heading for the house.

"Hey, Lena. Have you seen Zach?" I asked.

Lena smirked. "Oh, yeah," she said, pointing. "He's right over there."

I turned around, all smiles, and everything inside me dropped. There, standing behind the outdoor bar, grinning and sipping a beer, was my boyfriend. And pressing her huge boobs up against him while whispering flirtatiously into his ear was none other than Melanie Faison, my arch-rival.

five

My first instinct was to turn around and go back inside. Regroup. Maybe get my heart to stop trying to jackhammer its way out of my body. But the basketball players had already put their drinking game on pause; they were standing there, just waiting to see what I would do next. No way could I let them see me squirm.

I was not upset. I was a cool, confident girl. Or hoped I looked like one.

I tossed my hair back and sauntered to the bar. Neither Zach nor Melanie noticed me until I slapped my purse down on the glass-topped counter. They both glanced up, startled, and Zach turned white as snow.

"Hi, bartender. I think I'll have what she's having," I said.

Melanie smirked, and Zach practically shoved her

away from him. She took it well, lifting her blond curls over her wide shoulders and taking a sip of her beer.

"Noelle!" Zach said. "What are you doing here?"

"I came to surprise you," I told him. I glanced at Melanie, who had yet to retreat as any normal girl would have. "And clearly I have."

Zach looked from me to Melanie and laughed in a sort of halting way.

Melanie rolled her eyes. "It's not like we were *doing* anything," she said.

"Oh, really?" I replied. "Because it looked to me like you were all over my boyfriend."

I could feel the other backyard partyers watching us. More people poured out the back door, having been informed that some kind of drama was unfolding. I hated being the center of attention, but if I was going to be, I wasn't about to play the part of the whimpering girl-friend.

"We see what we want to see," Melanie said, lifting one shoulder.

"What the hell does that even mean?" I snapped.

"Noelle, calm down," Zach said quietly. "We were just . . . you know . . . talking."

"Funny. Last time I checked, a girl's boobs didn't have to be pushed into your chest for you to have a chat," I said.

"Ooooh," a few of the guys behind me intoned.

"Feeling inadequate?" Melanie asked, looking at my chest.

"Mel," Zach said in a scolding tone.

My eyes widened. "Mel? You're calling her *Mel*?" I blurted.

Suddenly a thousand awful thoughts flooded my brain. That night Zach hadn't shown up at the Bean because he was "sick." The way he'd talked as if he knew Melanie's game so well. Were these two really just talking, or was something going on between them?

"Noelle, calm down," Zach said, paling more and more by the second. "Let's go inside and talk about this."

"No. We're not going anywhere," I said. He reached for me, and I slapped his hand away.

"Noelle. Come on. You're making a scene," he said, glancing around.

"I'm making a scene? What about you? You're the one humiliating me in front of everyone!" I said angrily. "How do you think this looks?"

"Like he was trying to have a little fun for once?" Melanie suggested snottily.

Zach bowed his head and rubbed his face with his hands, as if he wanted to be anywhere but here.

"Who the hell do you think you are?" I snapped at Melanie.

"Noelle . . . " Zach pleaded.

"I don't know. Zach?" Melanie said, staring at him. Staring at him as if she had some claim on him. "Who am I, exactly?"

"What?" Zach said.

"Well, she's your girlfriend, right? So who am I?"

I was going to vomit. I really was.

"I have to get out of here," I said.

"Noelle, don't," Zach pleaded.

He grabbed my wrist, and I felt as if my skin was burning.

"If you don't want me to go, then tell me what the *hell* is going on here!" I shouted at him.

Just then the back door opened, and Danielle and Aurora came barreling out.

"What's going on?" Danielle asked as they flanked me.

I held a hand up. There was no way I could answer them. I was too busy trying not to burst into angry, hurt, humiliated tears.

"Look. Mel and I were just having a little fun," Zach explained, driving daggers into my chest. "Hanging out."

"Oh, what? I'm so un-fun you have to hang out with *her*?" I blurted. "Nice argument, Zach. How pathetic are you?"

Zach blinked, stung. "Well, it's not like you're ever around. What am I supposed to do while you're at your precious little coffeehouse all the time? Sit on my hands at home and think about how much I love my uptight girlfriend?"

"'Uptight'!? Well, at least I'm not a sorry-ass cliché!" I shouted, angry tears burning my eyes. "The totally oversexed, immature jock with an ego the size of Chicago!? Oh, where have I seen that before? Wait! I know! Every single teen movie ever made!"

"Damn. That's cold," one of the guys behind me said.

Now it was Zach's turn to be taken aback. Good. If you can dish it out, you'd better be able to take it, right?

"You know, I was going to wait until we were alone tomorrow to break up with you," Zach said icily. "But I think I'll just get it over with now. We're done, Noelle."

This was not happening. This was *not* happening.

"Fine!" I shouted at him, flipping into autopilot in an effort at self-preservation. "I couldn't look at you for two more seconds anyway."

"Great!"

"Great!"

With nothing left to do, I turned and stormed back into the party, my two best friends at my sides.

Monday was the worst day of my life. At least at home all day on Sunday I could cry and mope and lie in bed with the covers over my head, and no one knew the difference. But in the halls of Jefferson High School I was on display. Everywhere I went, girls looked at me with wide, sad, almost stunned eyes. Guys whispered behind their hands. It seemed as if no one could stop staring at me.

As I walked into the cafeteria for lunch, I tried not to breathe in the smells of the overcooked food. This was going to be the toughest hour of the day. I had to get through it without throwing up. I knew that if I ran for the bathroom, it would just feed the gossip fire that much more.

"Did you hear who's going to the prom together?" some junior girl asked her friend as I walked behind them. "Tammy Frankel and Mike Maldanno. Can you believe it?"

"I just hope someone asks me," her friend replied. "I

would kill to go to the senior prom."

My stomach turned, and they instantly clammed up as I edged past them. Adding insult to injury, prom tickets had gone on sale that morning, and it was all anyone could talk about—other than my tabloid-worthy breakup. Every time I thought about the prom, I wanted to burst into tears. For years I had been fantasizing about what the night would be like for me and Zach. I mean, once we'd been voted Class Couple, I knew we had a good shot at prom king and queen— so for the past few months I had imagined us out there for the spotlight dancing in our crowns as cameras flashed away. Now there was a good chance I wouldn't even have a date, let alone a crown.

How on earth had everything gotten so messed up?

"I wonder who Zach Miller will go with now that he and Noelle are no more," Mara Park said as I passed her table.

Bile rose up in my throat. I swallowed it back. Her friends all hushed her when they saw me, then whispered excitedly once I was out of earshot. I dropped down into the last chair at my usual table and slumped. There was only so much of this I could take.

"You okay, sweetie?" Aurora asked, touching my hand with her ringed fingers.

"Yeah," I lied. "Where's Zach?"

"He's sitting with Luke and those guys," Danielle said with a sympathetic gaze.

"Major downgrade if you ask me," Aurora said, taking a bite of her deli sandwich.

I forced a weak smile. "Thanks."

"Oh, *mija*. Why don't you just go talk to him?" Danielle suggested. "This is silly already."

"Danielle! He broke up with her in front of half the school!" Aurora said. "I vote she never talks to him again."

"So? Me and Jonah break up all the time! Big deal! Okay. So you had a huge fight. Who doesn't fight?" Danielle said, waving her pudding spoon around. "All he did was flirt a little. Everyone does that. *I* do that."

"You do?" Jonah asked as he joined us with a heaping tray of food.

"Like you don't know that," Danielle said.

"Yeah, but he was flirting with Melanie Faison," I told her. The very thought still made me sick. It wasn't just a betrayal. It was serious treachery. Zach *knew* how much I loathed that girl. "He could have picked anyone to flirt with. Why her?"

"Exactly," Aurora said.

"Besides, it wasn't just one fight," I told them, squirming slightly in my seat. I picked at the end of the metal coil on one of my notebooks. "We've been tense on and off for a while."

"You have?" Danielle asked.

"Yeah. I just . . . haven't talked about it," I said with a sigh. "I mean, you heard him. He said he was going to break up with me anyway. I am *not* going to go over there and, like, beg him to take me back."

At that moment, two tables away, Zach laughed, loud and mirthfully. I couldn't help but feel that had been for my benefit.

Look at me, babe. You're over there sick to your stomach, and I am just fine.

"Can we drop it?" I asked. "Let's talk about something else."

"I am all for that," Jonah mumbled through a mouthful of food.

Danielle whacked his arm, and he shrugged as if to say, *What?* But he had a point. I was impressed he was even still sitting with us while his best friend was with the other guys. It was a testament to how much he loved Danielle. I didn't want to punish him by making him listen to all this touchy-feely junk. Plus, I didn't need him going back to Zach and telling him that all I'd done during lunch was whine about our breakup.

"Are you gonna eat anything?" Aurora asked.

"Not hungry," I told her.

"Noelle, you gotta eat," Danielle said. "You have to keep your strength up for your match this week."

Right. My match. Irony to end all ironies, Melanie and I would be meeting in our first match of the season that Friday after school. Just thinking about it made my stomach turn all over again. One more laugh from Zach, and I was on my feet.

"I'm gonna go to the library," I said. "I can't take this."

"Here. Eat my cookie or something," Aurora offered, holding up a chocolate chip.

I grabbed it from her, just because I knew she wouldn't drop the subject otherwise, and speed-walked out of the room. I could feel everyone watching me, and I walked faster. This was going to be the longest week of my life.

She was killing me. Beating me into the court. I could return nothing. I was pathetic. A pathetic, talentless scrub. And she was loving every minute of it.

"Come on, Noelle!" Danielle shouted from the sidelines. "Focus! You can do this!"

I wanted to believe her. I did. But all I could feel was the heat of the sun on my neck. The beads of sweat on my skin. My exhausted, quivering muscles. I had been counting on adrenaline to take me through this and spur me to victory. At the very least I should have had karma on my side. Since Melanie had done in my relationship, the least the universe could do was grant me a win.

But my adrenaline was nil. And I was *so* tired. And Zach was there. Zach was there, rooting for *her*.

"Let's go, Mel!" he shouted. "One more point."

God, I hated him. I hated him with every fiber of my being.

On the far side of the court Melanie lifted her racket and served. I was too tired. I just wanted this to be over. So I did the unthinkable. I didn't even try.

"Game! Set! Match! Faison!" the ref shouted.

My team groaned. There went my undefeated season. On the other side of the net Melanie did her back handspring. I turned and walked off the court.

"Bairstow! Where are you going? Handshake!" Coach called after me.

I ignored her. I grabbed my duffel and tennis bag, shoved my racket into it, and turned for the parking lot. Out of the corner of my eye I could see Zach and Melanie hugging. If they kissed, I would hurl. Or faint. Or explode. I had to get out of there.

"Noelle! Wait up!" Danielle shouted after me. "You and me, we're going out tonight."

I laughed harshly. "No. We're not."

"Yes, we are!" she said, grabbing my arm and stopping me in my tracks.

I looked at the sky and sighed. Did she not see how tired and upset and completely freaked I was?

"Danielle, I just lost my first match of the season to the girl who just stole my boyfriend—"

"*Ex*-boyfriend," she corrected.

"Okay, ouch."

"I'm just saying!" Danielle told me as we started walking again. "It's good he's your ex, because he's clearly a jerk. And what do we do to ex-boyfriends-slash-jerks? We get revenge. And what's the best revenge? *Having fun!*"

"You've really thought this out, haven't you?" I breathed shakily, finally arriving at the door of my Ford Fusion. "I thought you wanted me to make up with him."

"Not anymore. Not after he showed up to cheer for that slut," Danielle stated, crossing her arms over her chest as I shoved my things into the backseat. "Look, you cannot keep wallowing like this. It's time to move on! Zach obviously has."

I slammed the front seat back into place and looked at her over the roof of the car. "Are you *trying* to hurt me?"

"No. I'm just trying to rile you up," Danielle said,

rushing around the car. She took my wrists and assumed the begging position. "Come on, Noelle. Come out with me and have a little fun!"

I shook my head miserably. "I just can't," I told her. "Wherever we go, there's a good chance *he'll* be there—don't you get that? And I don't want to be around him and his stupid friends right now. I just want to be alone."

"Noelle—"

God. Why wouldn't she stop? I collapsed into the front seat of the car and looked up at her, pleading with my eyes. "Danielle, I'm tired, okay? I want to go home," I said, feeling entirely drained.

Finally Danielle backed off. "Okay," she said, closing the door for me. "Call me if you need me."

"I will," I said.

Then I got out of there as fast as the speed limit would allow.

"See, now *this* is why I am anti-monogamy," my sister informed me on the phone that night.

"Wait. So you approve of Zach's potentially hooking up with another girl, like, five days after we broke up?" I asked, staring at the dark purple canopy over my bed.

"No. Of course not. I just mean that if you had never tied yourself down to Zach, you wouldn't be feeling this way now."

I sighed and pulled over another velvet throw pillow to prop my head up. My sister had a point. But would I really want to give up the past three years with Zach just so that

I wouldn't feel like crap now?

Yeah. Probably. At least I would have been right *then*.

"Look, you don't *need* a guy, Noelle," my sister said vehemently. I imagined her pacing her tiny dorm room wearing her signature head-to-toe black, her dyed-mahogany hair back in a tight bun, and her black-rimmed glasses perched on her nose. "None of us need men to complete us. That's just a line we're sold by society so that we continue to procreate and preserve the human race's eminent domain over our precious planet."

"Thanks, Faith. You really have a way of putting things into perspective," I answered wryly.

"Don't I?" she said, impressed with herself.

At that moment the door to my bedroom flew open, knocking my framed class picture off the wall. All the other plaques and photos shook, and I cringed, hoping nothing would smash.

"Way to make an entrance, Aurora," I said.

"It's my special talent," she answered.

She was wearing a pleated skirt over fishnets, platform shoes, and an extra layer of plum lipstick. Someone was dressed to party. This did not bode well.

"Get up! We're going out!" she said, walking over to me and yanking on my silk comforter. I screeched and almost fell off the bed but grabbed one of the bedposts just in time to save myself.

"Who is that? Is that Aurora?" my sister said with glee. "Tell her I said hi! I miss that little terror."

"Uh, I'm kind of on the phone," I told Aurora.

"So hang up," Aurora said.

"No," I replied.

"Hello? I'm kidnapping you! You have to do what I tell you to do," she told me, hands on hips.

"She's kidnapping you?" my sister cried. "Great! Perfect! Go out and *do* something!"

"Wait," I told Faith. I covered the receiver with one hand and sat up to glare at Aurora. "I appreciate the effort, but I am not in the mood to be kidnapped."

"Like that ever matters in a kidnapping." Aurora grunted impatiently. She went to my dresser and started randomly pulling out clothes. "Danielle told me you didn't want to go out with her and the jock jackasses, so I thought I'd take you out with *my* peeps."

"Your peeps?" I asked warily, watching as she started laying out an outfit for me.

"The drama club crowd," she said. "It'll be good for you to hang with some new people. You know, people with *souls*."

I almost laughed. There was no resisting Aurora's infectious energy. On the other end of the phone line Faith was shouting for my attention.

"What are you yelling about?" I asked her, lifting the phone again.

"Go with her! Go out!" Faith commanded.

"How did you even hear that?" I asked her.

"I was a dog in a former life. Come on, Noelle. This is exactly what you need," Faith urged me. "Please do not turn me into a cheerleader over here."

My brow creased. "Huh?"

"Go! Go, go, go!" she shouted.

She did sound a bit rah-rah-esque. "Okay! Okay! Stop before you strain something," I told her. "I'll go."

"Yeah, you will!" Aurora cheered.

"Yes!" Faith replied. "Call me when you get back. I don't care what time. The lit mag meeting's probably gonna go late anyway."

"You're going to a lit mag meeting on a Friday night?" I asked.

Faith groaned. "All the better reason for me to live vicariously through my little sister, right? Okay. Love ya, bye."

I hung up with Faith and glanced down at the clothes Aurora had laid out for me: a denim mini with black striped tights, a graphic T-shirt, and clunky black shoes.

"I don't know—"

"I'm the kidnapper," Aurora cut in. "So get dressed or die."

I sighed dramatically and took the clothes into my bathroom. This was going to be interesting.

six

"Nothing like the bowling alley on a Friday night," Aurora proclaimed, shoving open the glass doors and taking a deep breath. "Smell that stale, smoky air."

I took a deep breath and coughed so hard, my eyes almost popped out. "Yeah. That's good stuff."

Aurora peered around and grabbed me by the hand, her blue eyes twinkling in a mildly suspicious way. "C'mon. Let's get some shoes!"

She dragged me over to the high, wood-paneled counter where a couple of kids from school were already waiting. I vaguely recognized them from one of Aurora's plays and smiled.

"Hey! Trent! You're here! I didn't know you were coming!" Aurora announced grandly, slinging an arm around the shoulders of a tall, slim guy.

"Uh, you invited me," Trent said, clearly confused.

"That's right! I did, didn't I?" Aurora said, slapping his chest and turning him around to face me. "Trent, this is Noelle. Noelle, this is Trent."

Wow. Very subtle, Aurora. Could she make it any more obvious that this was a setup? Embarrassed, I smiled at Trent, and he smiled back. He *was* very cute—in an innocent, soulful way, with kind blue eyes and blond hair that sort of stuck out in all directions. He was wearing a green army jacket over a faded AIDS Walk T-shirt and had on half a dozen rubber bracelets of all colors and causes.

"Hi," I said. "You're the one who started up the Save Our Planet club last year, right?"

The school paper had done a story about him. Trent Davis was a junior now, but he had founded the environmental awareness club as a sophomore, then spent this year getting our rival school to form a chapter. Zach and his buddies called the kids in Save Our Planet the "sops" for short, always using a sarcastic sneer, but I thought it was pretty cool that someone at our school had that kind of initiative.

"Yeah. That was me," he said a bit sheepishly.

"See? You're famous!" Aurora exclaimed. "You guys get shoes. I'm gonna go program the scoreboard."

She bounded over to a group of similarly dressed girls who had commandeered a couple of lanes, leaving Trent and me alone. I gave the beefy, white-haired guy behind the counter my shoe size and averted my gaze from Trent, unsure what to say. How could Aurora do this to me? She had to know I wasn't ready to date.

"So, do you bowl much?" Trent asked finally.

"Not really," I said. "I'm sure I'm about to humiliate myself out there."

"Nah. You seem like one of those girls who succeeds at everything she does," he replied.

I flushed at the compliment. "Really?"

"Noelle Bairstow, valedictorian, tennis pro, Princeton-bound," he said as he paid for both pairs of shoes. He didn't even give me a chance to reach for my wallet. "Not a bad track record."

"You've done your homework," I said, relaxing a little.

Trent shrugged. "Didn't have to. Everyone knows who you are."

Okay, he was frank. That was new and different. And kind of pleasant, actually.

The guy behind the counter placed two pairs of shoes in front of us, then he sat back on a stool and reached for an aerosol can and a pair of freshly returned shoes.

"You know, every time you use that thing, the hole in the ozone layer grows," Trent mentioned.

Oh, God. Did he really just say that? The guy stared at Trent as if he had to be kidding.

"Would you rather have fungus-infested shoes that smell like toe jam?" the man asked.

"No. I'd rather you use a non-aerosol disinfectant wipe and maybe some all-natural shoe sachets," Trent told him.

The guy looked at me. "Is this kid for real?"

I stared back, my heart pounding. I could either defend Trent or slink off. I decided to be brave.

"A good lavender sachet kills pretty much any stench," I said, looking the guy steadily in the eye. "And with this skin, I need the ozone layer more than you know."

Trent grinned. A sizzle of attraction buzzed through me, surprising me a little.

"You know your stuff, Noelle," Trent said.

"I like the environment as much as the next girl," I answered with a flutter of pride. "Besides, I spend half my money on sunscreen. Do you realize the damage I could do at Marshall Field's with all that extra cash?"

Trent laughed.

"Enough." The man slammed his beefy hands onto the counter and stared us down. "How about this? You two granola-heads figure out a way for me to cut my budget in half and double my profits, and then maybe I'll be able to afford the fancy wipes and sachets. Until then, get outta my face."

Trent nodded and looked at me. "All right, then. Shall we?"

As we walked away I snorted a laugh. "Uh, yeah. I can't believe I just did that!"

"Hey, good for you. You're not gonna change the world by keeping your mouth shut," he said.

"True, but we won't be *around* to change it if we get our butts kicked by a guy like that," I shot back.

"A fair argument," Trent agreed diplomatically.

I dug around in my bag for my wallet and pulled out a

few dollars, holding them out to him.

"What's that for?" he asked.

"My shoes," I told him.

He paused in front of the snack bar and tilted his head with a smile. "How about you buy me fries and we'll call it even?" He glanced over his shoulder at Aurora and the others. "Last time I was here, I bowled a sixty."

"Is a sixty bad?" I asked.

Trent smirked. "Yeah. We're definitely not bowlers." He placed a hand on the small of my back, and another tingle passed through me. I almost tripped in surprise as he led me over to the vinyl-covered snack bar stools. I was happy to get off my suddenly shaky knees.

"I want to hear about Princeton," Trent said. "I'm thinking about applying there next year."

"Yeah?" I said, sliding onto a stool.

"Yeah. I figure if I can keep my grades up, win student body president at the end of the year, and maybe grow Save Our Planet to a few more local schools, there's no way they can turn me down."

"I'm impressed," I told him, pulling one of the little cardboard menus toward me.

"By what?" he asked.

"Just . . . you've thought a lot about your future."

"Who doesn't?" Trent asked.

Oh, I don't know. Guys who think their football skills are automatically going to take them everywhere in life?

"Some people," I told him.

"But not us," he said, elbowing me lightly.

"No," I said with a smile. I glanced at Aurora, who was watching us. She grinned and quickly looked away. I couldn't help but think that she'd done a good job picking out a potential new guy for me. Even if part of me still did want to kill her for going behind my back. "Not us."

"Dude, you are *so* wrong! The state shouldn't have the right to carve up parkland and just hand it out to whomever they want," Trent said vehemently.

"Uh, yeah, they should. It's a *state* park," his friend Morgan retorted.

"Right. It belongs to the *people* of the state. They should let the voters decide what to do with it in November," Trent said.

I took a deep breath of the warm morning air and looked at Trent admiringly. He was so passionate, so sure of himself. When he started to argue his point, his cheeks grew pink with effort, and a cute little line formed above his nose.

It was Monday morning after our Friday-night get-together, and we were all standing outside in front of the school before homeroom. I had seen Trent hanging with his friends on my way in and had stopped to say hello. A few of them looked at me with surprise at first, but now they seemed to have forgotten I was even there.

"Maybe we should petition the state senate," one of the girls piped up.

"Yeah. Cuz that always works," Trent said. "No. We have to do something more drastic this time."

"Like what?" I asked.

"I don't know yet," Trent told me. "But we can talk about it at our next meeting."

Out of the corner of my eye I saw a familiar figure, and my heart slammed to a halt. Zach—along with Jonah, Luke, and a couple of other guys—was approaching from the parking lot, talking and laughing. Why did Zach have to look so amazing in his favorite heather-gray Cubs T-shirt? His hair was slightly mussed. His arms were all tan, probably from a weekend in the sun playing flag football. I couldn't believe I was never going to be in those arms again. Had Melanie been? Had he hung out with her over the weekend?

I glanced at Trent. He was arguing some new point. Zach was rapidly approaching. On impulse I leaned into Trent's side and he looked at me, surprised. He smiled, then lifted his arm and placed it around my back before continuing his speech.

Perfect.

My heart pounded like crazy in my chest. Zach was ten feet away . . . eight . . . seven. Luke nudged Zach's arm and lifted his chin toward me and Trent. Zach looked up and completely blanched. He kept walking, but his stride stiffened, and he stared at us all the way through the front door.

Take that, Faison-lover. You're not the only one who can move on. Suddenly I felt light as air.

The first bell rang, and everyone got ready to go inside. Trent slipped his hand into mine and squeezed. "Listen, there's this art show over at the college this weekend," he told me, swinging our hands slightly. "I was wondering if you wanted to check it out with me on Saturday. I heard there's going to be some real wave-making work there."

Saturday. Saturday was no good. I had to work a double shift at the Magic Bean. All day. All night.

I glanced at Trent as we walked into the lobby. He looked so hopeful. A sour rush of trepidation overcame me. What if I said no, and he never asked again? What if he thought I wasn't interested, and he backed off? I didn't think I could handle that kind of rejection just now. Plus, I liked the feeling of his arm around me, his hand in mine. I liked it a lot.

"Uh, sure," I said finally, my brain screaming at me that I was nuts. "Sounds cool."

"Great," Trent said with a grin. A grin that made the trepidation disappear.

We walked up to the main hall and split—with me heading for the senior lockers, him heading for the junior hall. This was no problem. I would just have to find someone to cover my shift. A double. On a Saturday.

Yeah, right.

Saturday was an absolutely gorgeous warm spring day. It was sunny and breezy, and flowers were in bloom all over campus. It was the kind of day that made starting over actually seem possible. I'd have to remember to thank Ryan profusely for taking my shift. This might have been the best thing I could have done for myself.

Trent took me by the hand as we ducked past a college kid selling colorful helium balloons. Just to make the day that much more perfect, there was some kind of spring festival being held on campus. People were everywhere: eating ice cream, buying crafts from vendors all along the quad. A huge stage was set up for live music. All the school clubs, fraternities, and sororities were out in droves.

"This is so awesome," I said. "I can't wait to get to college."

"You're so lucky you get to go next year," Trent said, leading me down a pathway toward the campus art center. "I should have graduated early."

"But then you wouldn't be around to get all those new Save Our Planet chapters started," I reminded him.

"Good point," he said, squeezing my hand. "Hey. Hang on a sec."

He paused in front of a table set up near the entrance to the center. A cloth banner hung from the front that read SAVE OUR PARK! Sounded familiar.

"Hey, man," the dreadlocked guy behind the table greeted Trent, handing him a flyer. "There's a rally next weekend to stop the decimation of the state park by local developers. You should come."

"Hey. Is that the same thing you guys were talking about the other morning?" I asked Trent, taking a flyer for myself.

"Yeah. The state's letting these developers build all these high-rises on twenty acres that used to be reserved park space," Trent told me. "I've been talking about protesting with my environmental club," he explained to Mr. Dreadlocks.

"Righteous," Dreadlocks said with an appreciative nod. "You must be really proud of your boyfriend," he turned to me and said.

Both Trent and I blushed. "Yeah. I am," I replied. Correcting him would have been too messy.

"Will you come to the rally?" Dreadlocks's female counterpart asked us.

"Definitely. We'll be there," Trent assured them. "Right, Noelle?"

I blinked. Way to put me on the spot. I glanced at the flyer and the date didn't sound familiar. I was pretty sure I didn't have anything scheduled that night, but I felt all this pressure in my chest. Suddenly Trent was my boyfriend and automatically assuming we'd spend all this time together. . . .

Was it just me, or was this going a little fast? Did I want to get into a relationship situation so quickly? Or was I just overreacting? It wasn't as if Trent had asked me to be his girlfriend. Some random people had just assumed I was. I needed to chill.

"Noelle?" he said.

I realized I hadn't answered yet and that all three of them were staring at me expectantly. I couldn't exactly turn down my super-environmentalist "boyfriend" in front of these people, could I?

"Of course," I said. "I'll be there."

"Fantastic," Dreadlocks said with a huge smile. "Thanks

for caring, you guys. It's always nice to see kids your age getting involved."

Dude. You're only, like, a year older than me, I thought, but I let it slide. I just wanted to get inside and look at some art already. Trent shook hands with them and grabbed a few more flyers before finally leading the way into the art center.

Whew. Now our first real date could officially get started.

"Look at this one." Trent paused in front of a painting that was just a lot of red and purple slashes. "It's so . . . passionate."

"Really? I think it's sort of violent," I whispered.

"Yeah?" he asked, tilting his head and raising his eyebrows.

He nodded slightly, and that look of concentration came over him again. I smiled as I watched him take it all in. God, he was cute. And intelligent. And perceptive. He could stand and stare at a painting for fifteen minutes and interpret it in three different ways.

"Yeah, I can see that," he said finally, nodding. "There is a sort of angry vibe. But look." Then he pulled me to him, and we bumped hips as he slipped an arm around my back.

I blushed as another couple looked at us and smiled. They slipped out through a side door, leaving the two of us alone in the small gallery.

"See the rounding at the top?" Trent said. "And the

depth of the red in that part? Doesn't that make you think of love?"

My heart skipped a beat. I swallowed and looked up at his profile. Who knew guys like this existed? And at *my* school? If I had brought Zach here, he would have bailed half an hour ago to track down some beer and a Frisbee game out on the quad.

"Yeah," I answered. "I can see that, too."

Trent looked down at me and slowly smiled. It was as if he'd just realized how very close we were. Almost every part of our bodies were touching. Except our lips.

"Hey," he said, his gaze trailing from my eyes down to my mouth.

My heart pounded quick and shallow, and my skin tingled.

"Hey," I replied.

Then he lowered his lips to mine. My eyes fluttered closed and for a split second I froze up. I hadn't kissed anyone other than Zach, ever. This was just too weird. But then Trent turned fully toward me and slipped his hands around my waist. He deepened the kiss, and my breath caught. Trent—young, innocent-looking, earnest Trent— was good at this. *Really* good.

I circled his neck with my arms and pulled him even closer. Trent sighed with pleasure. I smiled and pulled away to look into his deep blue eyes. He wanted me. That much was clear. And in that moment I couldn't have wanted anyone more.

See? I wasn't uptight! I knew how to have fun. I had

kissed a guy in a public place! Maybe it just had to be the *right* guy.

Trent leaned in to kiss me again, and I completely let myself go. Suddenly Zach what's-his-name was nothing but a fading memory.

seven

"Can I help whoever's next?" I called out giddily. "I'm open over here!"

"Okay. What is *up* with you?" Ryan asked. He fired up the espresso machine behind me, talking over one shoulder as he worked the levers.

"I'm just in a really good mood," I said as I went to get a blueberry muffin for my next customer.

"That much is clear," he replied. "Your face looks like it was polished with Pledge. The question is, why?"

I picked up the muffin with some wax paper. "Actually, I have *you* to thank for it," I said, gesturing with the muffin. Some of the crumblies on top went flying, and a few sprayed him in the face. "Oops. Sorry."

"I'd like another one, please," the woman who had

ordered the muffin said flatly. "Those crunchy things are the best part."

"No problem!" I told her, slapping the muffin onto the back counter and grabbing another. Maybe I'd eat the rejected one myself later. I'd been a bottomless pit all week long.

Ryan laughed and shook his head at me. "Why are you thanking me for your current manic state?"

"Well, if you hadn't taken my shift on Saturday, then I never would have gone on that date, and if I hadn't gone on that date, he wouldn't have kissed me, and if he hadn't kissed me, I would not *be* in this manic state, as you call it."

Ryan looked at me as if I'd just told him that his mother died. All the playful mirth completely disappeared.

"What?" I demanded.

"What date?" he asked. "*Who* kissed you? Zach? You didn't get back together with that man-whore, did you?"

I laughed at the image of Zach as a man-whore and placed the muffin into a bag.

"No, I did not get back together with the *man-whore*." I whispered the last word, then I poured a coffee for Muffin Lady and handed her the finished order. "Three dollars, please!" I trilled.

"Then who was it?" Ryan asked. He crossed his arms over his chest and hovered behind me. "And this had better be good, because I missed SpringFest because of you, and if my bandmates' hangovers are any indication, it pretty much kicked ass."

Muffin Lady and I exchanged a wary look as I handed

back her change. Uh-oh. Was he *mad* at me? I slammed the register drawer closed and turned to face him.

"What's the matter?" I asked.

"Nothing. Just wondering who this random guy is that I haven't even heard about, who is apparently reaping the rewards of my double shift," he said.

I smiled at Ryan, touched. "That is so sweet."

"What's so sweet?"

"You're mad because I didn't tell you about him. You're right. I should keep my friends more in the loop."

Ryan stared at me. "Yeah. That's why I'm mad."

"I'm sorry I didn't tell you!" I said. "His name is Trent, and he's an amazing guy. I mean he's, like, an old soul, you know? He's into the environment and art, and he's hoping to go to Princeton. Anyway, he wanted to take me to this art exhibit at your school, and that was why I couldn't work on Saturday."

"Unbelievable," Ryan said, shaking his head and turning away.

"What? I'm sorry you missed SpringFest, okay? You didn't *have* to cover for me if you wanted to go that badly," I told him.

"It's not that!" he said, huffing a sigh. "It's just . . . a new guy? Already?"

I blinked and picked up a rag to wipe down the counter. "I know it's a little fast, but—"

"A little?" he cried. "Noelle, you are just setting yourself up to get slammed all over again."

My heart dropped, and I looked away, pretending to be

very intent on counter cleaning. "Why are you so freaked about this?" I asked, tucking a lock of hair behind my ear. "It's not like I don't know what I'm doing."

"I don't think you do," Ryan told me, lifting his hands. "Rebound relationships can be *really* messy, Noelle. Especially when you don't know the guy that well."

He's just concerned, I told myself. *And he's sweet to be concerned.* I just wished he wasn't so *adamant* about it. And loud. I could have done without the loud. Still, I smiled as I looked up at him.

"What?" he said flatly.

"You. I'm so lucky to have a friend like you," I told him, whacking his hip lightly with the rag. "And it's nice of you to care, really. But I'm *fine*. And I do know Trent."

Ryan's jaw clenched; I could see it popping out his cheek. "Yeah? How long have you known him?"

"A week and a half?"

Ryan threw his hands up.

"But that doesn't mean I don't *know* him!" I protested. "I swear, Ryan, now I can see all the compromises I made while I was dating Zach. I mean, who knew there were such mature, caring, artistic, *deep* guys out there?"

Ryan's nostrils flared slightly and he raised one hand. "Uh, I did," he said.

I laughed and shoved him away before turning to meet a couple of kids from school who had just stepped up to the register. Of course Ryan knew there were great guys out there. Being such a catch himself, he probably dated nothing *but* great guys. But for me Trent was a revelation and at the moment I just felt lucky that I was getting to know him.

And if Ryan was truly my friend, he should shut up and be happy for me.

Friday night I sat in the family room at Trent's house, cuddled into his side as he chuckled at *The Philadelphia Story*, some ancient black-and-white romantic comedy he had insisted on renting. I always thought it would be cool to watch one of these oldies—like it would make me feel cultured or something—but all this movie did was make me sleepy.

I mean, Katharine Hepburn was great, but I just could not figure out why all these men wanted her. Her character was so shrill and kind of cold. And—oh, God—they were singing again. A lot of singing for a non-musical . . .

Trent laughed, and my eyes popped open. I sat up a bit, embarrassed. I hadn't even realized I had dozed off.

"This movie is so hilarious," he said, reaching for the popcorn bowl on the coffee table. "Isn't it?"

"Yeah. Sure," I said, forcing a smile. The moment he turned away, I hid a yawn behind one hand. When was this thing gonna be over already?

"Oh, God. You're bored, aren't you?" Trent asked, catching me in the middle of my next, much bigger, yawn.

"No! No," I said. "I just . . . I guess I'm used to romantic comedies being a little . . . shorter."

"Aw, you just have to develop a taste for it," Trent said, putting a hand on my knee. "Jimmy Stewart was a comic *genius*."

He's no Steve Carell, I thought.

"Just give it a shot," Trent wheedled. "It's almost over anyway."

"Okay," I said with a reluctant smile.

His enthusiasm was kind of cute. I sat up straight and pulled my legs up under me, resolving to stay awake for the rest of the movie. Clearly Trent liked this stuff, and that's what couples did for each other—tried to appreciate the things the other person liked.

When Trent laughed, I laughed, too. I had entirely missed some joke, but I didn't want him to think I was totally lame. What was wrong with me? I was a smart girl. I couldn't get a little 1940s comedy?

Soon enough the movie was winding to a close, and Katharine was marrying not the guy she was engaged to and not the guy she had flirted with throughout the movie, but Cary Grant, her first husband, whom she had tossed out of her house in a rage at the very beginning of the film.

"See? Wasn't that romantic?" Trent asked, turning toward me.

Uh, no? I thought. But I told him, "If you say so."

He encircled me with his arms, and I leaned my chin on his shoulder, looking up at him. He was *so* cute. And his skin was absolutely perfect. I wondered if he got that from his vegetarian diet.

"All right, so you're not into the classics," he murmured. "I have to say, I'm disappointed. I was kind of hoping that would get you into a romantic mood."

"Oh, yeah?" I said, lifting my head. There was that

adorable frankness again.

He shrugged and smiled. "Guess I'll just have to do that myself."

My heart flipped over as he touched his lips to mine. He ran his fingertips down my cheek, and I felt these tingles all over my body again. I turned on the couch so that I could lay both my legs across his and drew him as close to me as possible. My pulse pounded in my ears as I grabbed at his T-shirt. It was like I couldn't get close enough. I never wanted to let him go.

Trent's kiss was so passionate, so searching, it made me want to melt. Kissing Zach had never been like this. Not even in the beginning. At least, I didn't remember its ever being like this. Which made me wonder, had Zach and I ever been in love? If kissing could feel this good, and it had never felt this good with him, how could it have possibly been love?

And if it wasn't love with Zach, did that mean that this *was* love?

I pulled away from Trent abruptly, gasping for air. Suddenly I felt confused and muddled and totally dizzy. Trent choked in a surprised breath. His chest heaved up and down under my fingertips.

"Sorry. Did I bite you or something?" he said, holding on to my other hand in my lap.

"No. No," I said with a laugh. I shook my head, trying to clear it. "I just got a little . . . overwhelmed."

Trent nodded. "Me, too. Kissing you is like—"

"I know," I said.

"You do?"

"Oh, yeah," I told him.

Trent smiled. "Cool."

Then he leaned in and kissed me again, pressing me back into the couch. Forget Zach and love and where this was all going. For now Trent was right. This was cool. Definitely, definitely cool.

As I drove home from Trent's, I sang along to the radio at the top of my lungs. All sorts of emotions were swirling around inside me. One minute I was giddy, thinking of Trent's kiss. The next I was depressed and guilt-ridden, thinking of Zach and questioning whether I had ever loved him. How could I betray three years of absolute certainty with him by doubting it now? Seconds later I was hopeful and happy again. I was going from smiling and laughing and singing, to almost crying and choking on the words, to smiling again.

If anyone had seen me, they definitely would have called a psych ward.

So you can imagine what my heart did when I pulled onto my street and saw Zach's Xterra parked at the curb in front of my house. I nearly drove right off the road and into Mrs. Splete's rhododendrons.

What the hell is he doing here? I wondered, somehow managing to pull my car into the driveway and *not* slam into the rear bumper of my mom's Saab.

I shifted into park and stared out the window. Zach was just standing up from the doorstep. To complicate matters, he looked drop-dead gorgeous. He was wearing the blue ribbed sweater I'd given him for his birthday.

Okay, just be strong. Whatever he says, do not *get emotional. Don't give him the satisfaction.*

I opened the car door and paused. My legs were shaking.

"Hey," he said, pushing his hands into the front pockets of his jeans. He actually looked tentative. My confident, cocky boyfriend looked tentative.

Ex-boyfriend.

"Hi." I managed to close the car door behind me.

"Where're you coming from?" he asked, glancing at my car.

Unbelievable. Keeping tabs? "Why are you here?" I asked him.

"Noelle, I'm so sorry," he said, his eyes steady as he took a few steps toward me on the front walk. "I didn't mean for any of this to happen. I was never remotely interested in Melanie, okay? It was all just . . . stupid."

Wow. On a sincerity scale of one to ten, this apology was headed directly for the two-hundred range. I'd never seen him stare at me like that.

"I love you *so* much, Noelle," he continued. "I don't know what I was thinking."

He was right in front of me now, and he looked even better close up. He'd let a little stubble grow out on his chin, which he *knew* was the sexiest thing in the world. He reached out and took one of my hands gently in his.

"Let's just forget this ever happened, okay?" he said, ducking down to meet my gaze. "We'll go to the prom together like we were supposed to. Everything can go back to normal."

Normal. God, I loved the sound of that. Normalcy was my thing. Normalcy, familiarity, predictability. I looked up into Zach's hazel eyes as I had done a million times before, and I felt myself start to cave. It would feel so good just to fall into those arms. The arms that had belonged to me for three straight years. What had I been thinking when I doubted that I ever loved him? This was my Zach. And, yeah, maybe he'd said some harsh things to me, but I'd said harsh things right back to him. And he was practically begging. That couldn't have been easy for him and his macho-man ego.

But do you really want to deal with that ego again? I asked myself. Especially when I had Trent—sweet, attentive Trent—who actually listened to me and respected my opinions? Trent, whose incredibly intense kiss was still lingering on my lips?

"Whaddaya say?" Zach asked with a smile, lifting my hand and entwining our fingers together. "Be my girl again?"

Part of me wanted to say yes. *Yes, yes, yes.* But when I thought about the heart-wrenching pain of the past couple of weeks, I hesitated. And Zach saw it. He knew me that well.

"What?" he said, his face falling.

"It's just . . . I'm kind of seeing someone," I answered, biting my lip. "You know . . . Trent Davis?"

Zach dropped my hand and took a step back. "You're gonna throw away three years for that *junior*? What does he have that I don't have?"

Everything inside me shut down. Zach couldn't have done a better job of exhibiting his faults if he tried. He was so condescending sometimes, so judgmental. And such a sore, sore loser.

Everyone has flaws, of course. It wasn't as if I hadn't known about Zach's forever. But now I didn't *have* to deal with them anymore.

"I'm sorry, Zach. I . . . I'm going to have to think about this," I told him.

Zach took a deep breath. For a split second I was sure he was going to shout at me, and I braced myself, but instead he shook his head and looked at the ground.

"If that's what you need," he said finally. "You know where to find me."

I sighed. "Thank you," I told him. I started past him but paused. "And for the record, I'm really sorry for those things I said to you at the party that night."

Zach looked up at me. I had never seen him so vulnerable. "Me, too, Noelle. Really sorry," he said.

"Thanks."

Then I turned and walked into my house, a little dizzy, a lot drained, and more confused than ever.

eight

"You guys, what am I going to do?" I wailed, slumping down in one of the cushy vinyl chairs at our kitchen table.

It was Saturday night, and I'd just gotten home from a long shift at the Bean. On the way home I had called Aurora and Danielle and asked them to grab some ice cream and come over for a crisis conversation. Luckily, Faith had also returned from school that afternoon, so I had a third sympathetic ear ready and waiting.

Aurora sighed and lifted her legs up so that her knees were squished between her body and the tabletop. Danielle pulled a pint of Ben & Jerry's toward her and took a big, heaping spoonful.

Faith grabbed another container out of the freezer and dropped down across from me, pulling off the lid.

"Personally, I think the answer is obvious," she said, shoveling some Chunky Monkey into her mouth. "It's called a threesome."

"Omigod," Danielle gasped, nearly choking on her own ice cream.

I grabbed a plastic spoon and threw it at Faith's head. She laughed as it bounced off her glasses and hit the floor.

"As much as I support Noelle's right to slutdom, I beg to differ," Aurora stated. "Trent is the clear choice here."

"You would say that. Trent's your boy!" Danielle protested.

"So, what, you'd rather have her get back together with Zach 'Flirting with the Enemy' Miller?" Aurora said, dropping her boots to the floor. "What is this, jock solidarity?"

"No! But he did apologize," Danielle pointed out, sitting up straight as well. "And, Noelle, you love him, right? You guys have been together forever. Just think, everything could go back to normal. All of us sitting together at lunch, going to the prom in the same limo . . . "

"Uh, actually, about that," Aurora said, holding up one finger. "I think me and Drake are going with his friends."

"What?" Danielle and I both cried.

"But we need three couples to pay for the limo!" Danielle wailed.

"Ah, high school," Faith said wistfully, leaning back in her chair with her ice cream. "I *so* don't miss it."

We ignored her.

"I know, but Drake wants to stick with his friends, and they're getting a party bus that sounds totally awesome,"

Aurora said, sounding sheepish. "You guys can find some-one else to go in with you, I'm sure."

"I don't believe this," Danielle said.

"Me neither. We've only had this plan in place since, like, ninth grade," I grumbled.

"Uh, I hate to point out the obvious, but the limo will be the least of your problems if baby sis here doesn't figure out who she's bringing," Faith said.

"Good point," I told her, dropping my head onto my folded arms. I couldn't take much more of this. Every time I thought about going to the prom with Zach, it felt so right. So perfect. But then I'd think about going with Trent, dancing close to him, kissing him in the back of the limo, and it felt right in a whole other way.

"I've got it!" Faith announced.

"Please tell me you actually *do* have it," I groaned.

"Hey, our parents don't pay the big bucks to send me to Northwestern for nothing," Faith said. "Why don't you take that hottie from the coffeehouse? What's his name . . . Brian . . . Ryan!"

Aurora, Danielle, and I all looked at one another and cracked up laughing.

"What!? You had a crush on him when you first started working there, right?" Faith pointed out. "And that boy is hot."

"Uh, yeah. He's also gay," I countered.

Faith's shoulders drooped. "You're kidding."

"Somewhere there's a guy walking around who has no idea that he's going to meet Ryan Corcoran and become the luckiest man on earth," Aurora said, shaking her head wistfully. "Sucks to be a girl."

"No doubt," Danielle added.

"All right, so, if we all agree that Ryan is great, then why don't you hold out for someone Ryan-like?" Faith suggested. "Just one who likes girls."

I snorted a laugh. "That might be a good plan, but prom tickets are only on sale for another week. I don't have that kind of time." I sat up straight and flattened my hands on the table. "Come on, you guys. We are four enlightened, intelligent, intuitive women."

"We are?" Aurora joked as she tried to stick her spoon to her nose.

"Yes! We are. And we can figure this out. So who's it gonna be? Trent or Zach?"

"Trent!" Aurora shouted.

"Zach!" Danielle shouted louder.

"I'll go with you," Faith offered.

I groaned, and my head hit the table again. This was definitely not helping.

Monday night I sat in the break room at the Magic Bean, staring at my untouched cup of coffee, my crossed leg jumping up and down under the tiny metal table. All day I had avoided Zach, ducking into empty classrooms or the bathroom whenever I happened to spot him in the hall. I knew that I was being totally unfair. I had to give him an answer. Sure, I could buy my own ticket to the prom, but if I chose Trent, I wanted to make sure Zach had enough time to buy *his* own ticket. After all, if I went with Trent, then Zach should still be able to go to his senior prom, right? I owed it to him to make a decision before Friday, when the administration would take the tickets off the market for good.

What was I going to do? Part of me wished I could turn back time to the night of the infamous party and just go to it with Zach. Then none of this would have happened. Of course, I wouldn't have kissed Trent either. . . .

The break room door opened and I jumped, slamming my knee into the underside of the table and spilling coffee everywhere.

"Ow! Damn!"

It was Ryan. "Omigod. Are you okay?" he asked, grabbing a towel from a shelf to clean up the spill.

"Yeah, I'm fine." I rubbed my knee. "Is my fifteen over already?"

"No. I was just coming back for more sugar," he told me. His brow creased as he looked down at me. "You okay? You look kind of tense."

"I am tense," I admitted, standing. "Zach asked me to the prom."

"What?" Ryan blurted.

"Yeah! I know! I was about two seconds from asking Trent to go with me, and then Zach shows up at my house and gives me this perfect apology and asks me to go with him! And, I mean, I do still love him . . . I think. But Trent is *so* sweet and amazing. But then I have all that history with Zach—"

"That's it," Ryan said, throwing the towel down. "I can't take this anymore."

And then he grabbed my face and kissed me.

Shocked, I leaned back against the metal shelves behind me. Toilet paper rolls rained down from above and bounced along the tile floor.

Ryan is kissing me. Ryan is kissing me! What the hell—?

Just then, the door opened again, and Ryan and I sprang apart. Mitch stood there, jacket in hand, gaping at us.

"Well, it's about time," he said.

"What . . . what . . . "

My heart was swirling in one direction, and my brain was swirling in the exact opposite. I tried to bring my hands to my head, but I was so off balance, I smacked myself in the nose.

"Are you okay?" Ryan asked me.

"But you're gay!" I cried.

"What?" Ryan demanded. He and Mitch looked at each other.

"Honey, I *wish*," Mitch said, laughing as he shoved his time card into the slot.

"Where the hell did you get that idea?" Ryan asked me.

"Everyone said . . . I thought you . . . you're so . . . " I had absolutely no idea who he was now. "You're *not* gay?"

"I think I'm gonna get out of here before I get swept up in this maelstrom of delusion," Mitch said, slipping past us. He slapped Ryan twice on the shoulder. "Good luck."

Then he walked out, closing the door behind us and leaving Ryan and me alone.

"Who told you I was gay?" Ryan asked, crossing his arms over his chest.

I stumbled to the nearest chair and sat down, hard. "Everyone. When I first started working here, I told Jenna I thought you were cute, and she said, 'Keep dreaming,' and then Doris agreed with her." I looked up at him, wide-eyed. "Ryan, everyone who works here thinks you're gay."

Ryan stared back at me, half anxious, half bewildered. "Well. That's interesting. And you believed them?"

"Well . . . you were always hanging out with Mitch, and you were so sweet and such a good listener and a good dresser," I said, feeling pathetic. I closed my eyes and covered them with my hands. "Oh, God. I'm a bigot."

Ryan laughed. He walked over and crouched down in front of me. When I dared to peek, all I could see were his slightly tanned forearms resting on his thighs, his calloused fingers laced together.

"You're not a bigot," Ryan said, ducking his face into my line of vision. I looked up and sighed. "And, if I'm hearing correctly, you think I'm cute," he said. "You think I'm sweet, a good listener, and a good dresser. All good things for me."

I smiled, toying with my empty coffee cup. I found that I could not, for the life of me, look directly at him. My brain was still reeling from that unexpected kiss. And the fact that a huge part of who I'd thought he was had just been completely obliterated.

"What did Mitch mean when he said it was about time?" I asked finally, once I could breathe again.

Ryan cleared his throat. He hopped up and pulled the

other chair around the table, sitting so that his knees were almost touching mine.

"Well, I've kind of wanted to do that ever since I met you," he said.

My heart gave a little leap, and I finally glanced at him. He reached out and took one of my hands, drawing it toward him so that I had to turn and face him completely. I took a deep breath, staring down at our fingers.

"Why didn't you tell me sooner?" I asked quietly.

"You were always with Zach," he said. Then he exhaled in frustration. "But that shouldn't have mattered. I guess I'm just a wuss—I don't know. I'm telling you now."

Great, I thought. *Now I have* three *guys to choose from. As if I wasn't already confused enough.*

"Noelle, these guys . . . they have no idea what they have. Trust me," he said, his voice growing husky. "I know you better than anyone."

He had a point there. I did tell him *everything.* Even things I didn't tell Danielle and Aurora. He reached out and tipped my chin up with one finger, forcing me to look him in the eye. Those intense green eyes that were gazing at me as if I was the only girl on earth. How had I never noticed this before?

"Be with me," he said firmly. "At least . . . give me a shot."

Wow. What was I supposed to do with a plea like that from a guy like him? I felt as if my entire body was on fire.

But this was *Ryan.* One of my best friends. My beautiful best friend, yeah, but still. He knew everything about me and no matter what he thought, I wasn't entirely sure that was a good thing.

I took a deep breath and turned away. "I can't believe you're not into guys," I said with a laugh, trying to lighten the moment.

"I can't believe everyone thinks I am," he grumbled.

"Ryan . . . " I said tentatively.

"Uh-oh. That was not a good tone," he said.

"No! It's not that. It's just . . . I have to think about this. I mean, five minutes ago I thought you were my gay best friend, and now I find out you're not gay and you've liked me for, like, eight months. It's kind of a lot to process."

"I get it," he said, standing and wiping his palms on his jeans. "That's fine. I . . . understand."

"You're sure?"

"Yeah," he said with a quick smile. "What do you say we walk out of here and work the rest of our shift and act like nothing happened?"

"Sounds good," I replied, relieved.

"Okay." He grabbed a sack of sugar and turned for the door but paused. "Just . . . let me know what you decide."

"I will," I told him.

He closed the door quietly behind him, and I stared at it for a good five minutes, my pulse still racing at an unhealthy rate.

Ryan Corcoran had kissed me. Ryan Corcoran was not gay. Ryan Corcoran was, in fact, totally into me.

What the hell was I going to do now?

✳ ✳ ✳

Tuesday morning between third and fourth period, I made my way on shaky legs to the home ec room in a back corner of the school. Mrs. Lane, our class advisor, was in charge of doling out the prom tickets, and I had decided it was high time I buy my own. If only I knew who I was going to go with.

I was just about to round the corner when Trent stepped out of the guidance office with a stack of flyers in his hand. I froze. He wore a black T-shirt and a necklace made of small wooden beads. His hair, as always, stuck out adorably in all directions.

"Hey!" he said happily, giving me a kiss on the cheek. "Where are you going?"

"Uh . . . to the nurse," I said, improvising.

Trent immediately grew concerned. "Are you okay?" he asked, reaching for my hand.

"Yeah, fine," I said. I pulled away quickly. "Just a little headache. I'm gonna get some Tylenol."

"You know, ninety-seven percent of headaches are caused by simple dehydration," he told me. "Maybe you need some water."

I forced a smile. "This one's bigger than water."

"Still, you shouldn't put chemicals into your body unless you really need them to—"

"What were you doing in there?" I interrupted, lifting my chin at the office.

"Oh, I'm putting these up all over school," Trent said, showing me dozens of copies of the sheet he'd been given at the college a couple of weeks ago. "My goal is to get at least a hundred kids from Jefferson to go."

"Right," I said with a nod. Amid all the prom talk I'd completely forgotten about the rally.

"You're still coming, right?" he asked.

"Oh, yeah. Definitely," I told him. *If you still want me to go with you, after I ask Zach to the prom. Or Ryan. Or maybe I'll pick you and we won't ever have to know.*

Now I *was* getting a headache.

"Feel better," he told me, giving me another quick kiss.

"Thanks."

Just then Zach stepped out of a classroom a bit farther down the main hall. He didn't see me, but I saw him, and it made my heart beat faster. These boys were everywhere. Thank God there was no chance of Ryan's coming around a corner. If I saw him just then, I might have popped a blood vessel.

I took a deep breath, turned around, and walked into Mrs. Lane's room. She was sitting at her desk, flipping through her planner.

"Hi, Mrs. Lane," I said weakly.

She looked up and smiled. "Noelle! I assume you're here for your prom tickets."

"Yep."

My heart pounded fast and shallow. I was taking the leap. Laying down the dough. And Zach, Trent, and Ryan might as well have all been there, staring me down.

"Go with me. It'll be just like old times."

"Noelle, go with me. I make your knees buckle."

"Give me a shot, Noelle. I'm your best friend."

Mrs. Lane lifted a lockbox out of her bottom drawer and opened it. I scrambled in my bag for the cash, then handed it over.

"Noelle Bairstow plus one," she said, making a note on her class list. She offered me a thick white envelope containing the prom tickets. "So?" she said, looking at me over her glasses. "Who's the lucky boy?"

I reached out with a shaky hand and took the envelope. It felt bizarrely heavy in my palm. I forced a smile.

Good question, Mrs. Lane. Really good question.

The Choice

$Okay,$ this is too much. I have never been this stressed in my life. Whatever I do, I'm going to hurt two people I care about, so I have to make sure that it's the right decision. No one can help me but you. Here are the candidates again:

1. Zach

Pros: We've been together forever, and we shared all those firsts. He's completely beautiful and athletic and mostly thoughtful, and I've always felt safe in his arms. Even though we fight sometimes, we always make up. Plus, we have a good shot at that whole prom king and queen thing, which would be sweet.

Cons: I'm not sure I can trust him anymore. He flirted with my archenemy in front of everyone, then came to that match to cheer for her. I know we had broken up, but that was cruel. And what did it mean? Were he and Melanie *together* while he and I were apart? The idea makes me want to vomit.

Heartbreak risk level: High

· ·

2. Trent

Pros: He's mature, passionate, and knows what he wants. And he is so, so sweet. I can't imagine his ever hurting me. And when he kisses me, I feel like I'm going to explode.

Cons: He's younger and can be kind of a know-it-all, telling people how to think and what to do. I'm not totally sure he would fit in with my friends at the prom. We also don't have that much in common. Except the kissing thing. Ah . . . the kissing . . .

Heartbreak risk level: Moderate

· ·

3. Ryan

Pros: Hot, hot, hottie. His kisses pretty much melt me. He's older, ridiculously sexy, and definitely mysterious. Plus, I've been crushing on him since sophomore year and now I finally have my shot. How could I pass that up?

Cons: He's older and has a lot of stuff going on with his band and everything. I'm not even entirely sure he'd be interested in going to a high school prom. There's also the issue of our friendship. If we did get together and it didn't work out, I would no longer be able to talk to the one person I *always* talk to. See the problem?

Heartbreak risk level: Severe

All right, it's decision-making time! This is my *senior prom,* so choose wisely. I'm going to remember this night for the rest of my life. And I want the memories to be good!

If you choose *Zach,* keep reading.

If you choose *Trent,* turn to page 151.

If you choose *Ryan,* turn to page 191.

You Chose Zach

nine

"Zach!" I shouted, jogging back into the hallway. He was still standing down by the science wing, chatting with Jonah. "Zach! Zach, Zach, Zach!"

I practically skipped right up to him, feeling lighter than puffed pastry now that I had finally made my decision. He and Jonah both stared at me like I was a bunny on speed.

"See what I just got?" I asked Zach, holding the prom tickets up.

"Prom tickets," he said flatly. Then his eyes widened, and he grinned. "Does that mean—?"

The glee on his face put any lingering doubts to rest. This was Zach. My boyfriend. The guy I was supposed to be with.

"Yeah," I said, nodding. "Let's go to the prom together."

"Yes!" Zach cheered. He grabbed me up in his strong arms and twirled me around. I squealed. A couple of junior girls had to jump out of the way of my legs.

"Thank *God*!" Jonah said dramatically.

Zach set me back down on the floor, and I smiled up at him.

"I love you so much," he said, giving me a quick but firm kiss.

"I love you, too," I told him.

Then we hugged again, and I closed my eyes, resting my cheek against his chest and inhaling the familiar scent of his fabric softener.

Oh yeah, this was right. This was good. This was exactly where I was supposed to be.

Of course, I still had to deal with Trent. The way gossip traveled at the speed of light around here, he'd know about the Class Couple's theatrical reunion before lunchtime. He had to hear it from me first. It was only right.

After English class I rushed for the second floor, hoping to catch Trent outside his history class. Luckily, he had stayed behind to debate some political position with Mr. Harris. He was the last student out of the room.

"Hi, Trent," I said, taking a deep breath as I stepped in front of him.

"Hey!" he said brightly, leaning in to kiss me.

I flinched away, my heart squeezing into a tight ball. Trent stood up straight and looked at me, confused.

"Are you okay?" he asked. "Still have that headache? Because I have a bottle of water if you—"

"Actually, I have to tell you something," I interrupted, glancing around, making sure no one was within earshot. The last thing I wanted was a ton of witnesses to another dramatic scene. "There's no easy way to say this. . . ."

"So just say it," Trent said with a shrug.

He did appreciate the up-front approach. "Okay. I'm getting back together with Zach."

All the color drained from Trent's face. For a split second I actually thought he might faint. Instead he blew out a breath and leaned back against the lockers.

"Oh."

"I'm really sorry, Trent," I apologized, and I meant it. "I've been having a great time with you."

"So have I," he told me. "What happened?"

I swallowed hard and hugged my books to my chest. "It's just . . . I love him."

"Oh," he said again, looking at the floor. "Well. This kind of sucks. I thought we really—I don't know—connected."

"We did," I told him, remembering all those intense kisses. "It's just, Zach and I—"

"I get it," he said. "You've gotta do what's right for you."

"Really?" I said with disbelief.

"Yeah." He managed to smile as he looked at me. "Thanks for being honest about it."

I was so touched I literally lost my breath for a second. Was he really thanking me while I broke up with him? I couldn't have been more stunned if he'd told me he was going to eat a big old hamburger. For a junior, Trent was definitely mature.

"Well, I guess I should go," I said lamely.

"Yeah. No need to drag this out," he told me, his eyes sympathetic as he stood up straight. "Good luck with everything. Princeton and all . . . "

"Thanks. You, too," I told him.

I turned and walked away, actually feeling good. Who knew a breakup could go that well? If only they were all like that. . . .

"To the Class Couple," Zach said, lifting his soda over the blue tablecloth. "Back together again."

I laughed and clinked my glass against his. "The way it should be."

We each sipped our drinks, looking goofily into each other's eyes. It was Friday night, and we were sitting at a small table at the Porch Light Grill, a steakhouse in the center of town. Zach had suggested the slightly out-of-our-normal-price-range venue for a reunion celebration, and I had taken him up on it instantly. The sooner things got back to normal, the better.

"You look beautiful tonight," Zach said, making me blush. "Your hair looks incredible like that."

I reached up and touched the silky curls that had been tickling my bare shoulders all evening. In addition to the new hairstyle, I'd gone with a blue strapless dress in honor of the occasion.

"Thanks. Faith did it," I told him. "Apparently she picked up more than big words at that school of hers."

"Faith is back, huh? I'm surprised she didn't come after me with a shotgun," he joked.

"She thought about it, but I told her I wouldn't appreciate it very much." I squirmed a little at this reference to our breakup. I didn't want to talk about it. All I wanted was to move on.

"Thanks for that," he said, leaning back as his appetizer—a huge plate of chili cheese fries—was placed in front of him. "Have I mentioned again how bad I feel? About everything?"

"You did," I replied gratefully.

He grabbed my bread plate and his fork and went about extricating all the chili-free French fries for me. If someone had told me last week that I would be here with Zach now, comfortably bantering and sharing a plate of fries (that he knew I wanted chili-free), I never would have believed it. I was so happy to be with him again. To be so chill and comfortable. To be looking forward to our prom again.

"Chili-free fries for my girl," he said, standing up slightly to kiss my forehead as he handed them over.

I took a deep breath and nibbled on a fry. Screw Melanie Faison. So they had flirted. Maybe even kissed. Big monster deal. Zach had simply suffered a moment of temporary insanity. Besides, I would bet my entire paycheck that *she* had come on to *him*. And who was I to pass judgment? I'd kissed two boys in the past week.

Things were a lot less tense now than they had been the

week before our breakup. Maybe that fight had been exactly what we needed. Maybe we had just been aching to get all that crap off our chests, and now that we had, things could be even better than before.

"So, what do you want to do after this?" Zach asked, scooping up some chili with a fry.

"I don't know. I was thinking maybe we should just go back to the basement and hang," I told him, infusing my words with meaning.

Zach didn't miss it. He looked up at me. "Yeah?"

"Yeah," I said with a smile.

"Check, please!" Zach joked, raising a hand.

I laughed and popped another fry into my mouth. It was good to be back where I belonged.

I could *feel* Ryan behind me as I placed an assortment of cookies on a plate at the pastry case. We had been working side by side for over an hour and had barely said two words to each other. The tension was coming off him like steam out of the cappuccino machine. I knew that I needed to tell him I had gotten back together with Zach, but every time I thought about it, my skin prickled with dread.

I closed the case and turned around with the plateful of cookies. At the exact same moment Ryan turned from the coffee machine, and we slammed right into each other. Cookies went flying, and steaming hot coffee sloshed over the rim of his cup.

"Sorry," I said, dropping to the floor to retrieve the snacks. "Sorry."

"My fault," he muttered, stepping awkwardly over me to wipe up the spill.

I dumped the cookies into the garbage, and my face burned as I went to put together another plate. Ryan and I had never been so out of sync. Not even during my first week of work. It was torture.

The front door opened, and Ryan and I both looked up. Strike my previous statement. Torture had just sauntered in the door.

Melanie Faison.

With overdone makeup and sass, she stared me down as she approached. Her halter top was so binding, she was practically choking on her cleavage. She slapped her beaded bag down on the counter, startling the customer who was waiting for her cookies.

Ryan glanced at me as Melanie glared. He could clearly tell something was up.

"May I help you?" he said to Melanie.

"No. I want to talk to *her*," Melanie said, arching an eyebrow. "And she knows it."

I shakily handed the woman her cookies. She wisely moved away.

"What can I do for you, Melanie?" I asked, steeling myself. I could do this. Whatever it was.

"Nothing. I just wanted to tell you to enjoy it while it lasts," she said haughtily. "It's not gonna be long before Zach gets bored with you again and comes running back to me."

I could feel Ryan's eyes boring into the side of my head.

109

So much for breaking the news gently. I attempted to swallow but almost choked instead. A few girls from school were sitting at a table near the counter and their conversation had ceased. They stared at one another, happy as pigs in mud to witness something so gossip-worthy.

"What do you mean, 'back to you'?" I said, amazed at the strength of my own voice. "It's not like you guys were together."

I hope? I hope, I hope, I hope.

Melanie sneered, her eyes darting over me as if she could not believe the stunning depth of my naïveté. "Yeah. You just keep telling yourself that."

All the blood in my body rushed to my toes. I placed my hands flat on the counter as my mind clouded over.

"Look, I came in here in the spirit of good sportsmanship," she added with faux sweetness. "I like my opponents to know what they're up against. So take a good look. Cuz you're up against all this." She flicked her hands toward her curvaceous bod.

I was going to throw up. Right here, right now. Which might be okay if I could get it all to land on *her*.

"All right, that's enough," Ryan cut in, stepping up next to me and staring Melanie down. "You can go."

Melanie looked him over and smiled flirtatiously. "A new knight for our damsel?" she said. "I'll give you this, Bairstow. You got good taste." Then she slid her bag off the counter, gave Ryan one last lascivious glance, and strode out.

Ryan took a deep breath and turned to face me. "Back

together with Zach, then, huh?"

I looked up at him, and the entire room tilted. That was all I needed. I turned around and hauled ass for the break room. I didn't even have time to close the bathroom door before my knees hit the floor and I heaved into the bowl. My eyes stung as my stomach clenched and my chest constricted. I heard the door open.

"Are you okay?"

"Get out!" I shouted, heaving again.

Ryan closed the outer door and disappeared. Once I was done, I groped for the bathroom door and shut that as well. Then I grabbed the rim of the sink and hoisted myself to my feet. I closed my eyes and flushed the toilet. I didn't want to see what I had done.

Okay. You're okay, I told myself, gripping the sides of the sink and pulling in a shaky breath.

I filled a paper cup with water and rinsed my mouth out. I looked at my red, watery eyes in the mirror. Yeah. Very attractive. At least I had waited until Melanie was gone.

I took another deep breath and leaned back shakily against the door, savoring the feeling of the cool metal against my hot skin. What the hell had actually gone on between Melanie and Zach? Had they fooled around? Had they . . . had sex?

Oh, God. My stomach turned again. I was the only person Zach had ever been with. And I'd just been with him again on Friday night. If I ever found out that he had slept with Melanie in between our anniversary and now—even if we were broken up at the time—I was going to die.

I pushed myself away from the wall and peered at my reflection again: wan face, my flat chest, my thin arms, and limp hair. Even without having just hovered over the toilet, I certainly didn't have Melanie's curves. Another horrifying thought came over me, and I braced my hands against the sink once more. If they had fooled around, if Zach *had* been attracted to her, then how could he possibly be attracted to me? Was Melanie Faison the kind of girl Zach really wanted?

ten

On Thursday night I parked my car in front of Zach's house and checked my reflection in the rearview mirror. Super-curled lashes? Check. More eyeliner than I've ever worn in my life? Check. Bright red lips that it was taking all my willpower not to wipe off on the back of my hand? Check.

If this was the kind of girl Zach wanted, this was the kind of girl I'd give him.

For one night, at least.

I took a deep breath and screwed up my courage. I had to do this. The last few days had been torture. No matter how many pep talks I'd given myself, I couldn't stop think-ing about what Melanie had said and wondering what it meant. I was tense all the time at school watching Zach and his friends, wondering what they were talking about—if they knew something I didn't. Every time Zach kissed me, I froze up, then realized I was freezing up and tried to relax.

Everything is fine, I kept telling myself. *Melanie Faison is a liar and a jerk, and she was just trying to get under your skin.*

Well, score one for Melanie. Because it worked.

But, little did she know, I was not going to back down that easily. Maybe she had beaten me in our first match of the season, but I was not going to let her beat me at this. This was far more important. This was Zach. He was mine, and I was going to keep him. If I had to fight fire with fire, then so be it.

So here I was, dressed all sexy and ready to give Zach the night of his life.

I got out of the car and straightened the tight skirt of my new, low-cut dress. Zach's parents were out of town on a business trip for a couple of nights, so I knew no one was home, but I still felt self-conscious as I teetered up the walk in my three-inch heels. I had to be six feet tall in these things—almost as tall as Zach. Which begged the question: Did I look sexy, or did I look like a slutty giraffe?

Okay, confidence, I reminded myself as I rang the door-bell. *Just . . . be sexy.*

Two seconds later, Zach opened the door, and his jaw literally dropped.

"Hey there," I said with a smile, putting my hands on my hips.

"Noelle?" he gasped.

I couldn't blame him for the shock. This *was* completely out of character.

Okay. Now what? Images from soap operas flitted through my mind. I decided to just go for it. I placed my hands on his shoulders, shoved him inside and up against a wall of the foyer, then laid a seriously deep kiss on him. Any second now I was going to crack up laughing from the absurdity of it all. Or he was. He had to see how ridiculous this was.

Except he didn't. In fact, he seemed to think it was absolute perfection. Zach slid his hands up and down my nearly bare back and pulled me close. I could feel that he was already, well, *ready*.

He ran a hand up my neck and grabbed hold of my curls. "God, you're sexy," he said, pulling away for a split second before trailing kisses down my neck. "Where did you get this dress? It's so *hot!*"

Out of nowhere a knot welled up in my throat.

So he did like this kind of girl. This sexy temptress thing. He'd never gotten excited that fast with just little old me in my sweats on the couch.

You're the one who decided to do this, Noelle, I told myself. *You can't get mad at him for going along with it.*

"Hey. You okay?" Zach asked, looking into my blinking eyes.

I forced a smile, took his hands, and leaned back, pulling him away from the wall. I had gotten myself into it. I had to see it through.

"Let's go upstairs," I said.

Zach smiled slowly and slipped a hand back under the blanket of my hair. "I love you so much," he said huskily.

You'd better, I thought as I led him up to his room. *You'd better.*

"Come on, Noelle! You can do it! Take this girl down already!" Danielle shouted at me from the bleachers at Crestwood High School.

"Let's go, Noelle!" Zach shouted. "Look alive!"

I gripped my racket and settled into my return stance. It was Friday afternoon, and all the top tennis players had gathered at one of the local schools for a round-robin to determine our seeding for the state championships. I had easily won my first match, but this new girl, Tanya Zurich, was giving me a bit of trouble.

The worst part was I couldn't figure out *why*. She wasn't a bad player, but she wasn't fast on her feet, and her serve speed was crap. Was I really so tired from my night with Zach that I couldn't rally and come back against this girl?

Maybe I'd be playing better if I had been able to eat more than half a plain bagel at lunch. I *knew* I'd have to play two matches this afternoon. I should have tried harder to get down some protein or at least a little juice. But my stomach just didn't want to eat, and the thought of getting sick before a game was even worse than the thought of not fueling up.

Just concentrate, I told myself. *You can do this.*

Tanya reached up to serve, and I held my breath. I envisioned exactly where the ball would land, and I went for it. But my timing was off, and my return shot was misplaced. It flew right to her instead of off her left foot, as I had planned. Tanya easily rocketed the ball back to the far side of the court. I ran for it, and, miraculously, my return shot made it over the net and fell like a stone. She had no chance to get there.

"Thirty, thirty," the ref announced.

Danielle and the others went wild.

I smiled in relief. Okay. Just a few more points. I could still win this. I looked up at my friends for a jolt of support and nearly tripped. I got a jolt all right, but not the one I was hoping for.

Melanie Faison stood at one side of the bleachers in her tiny tennis skirt, looking up at Zach, who was at the end of the top row. He wasn't looking at me, urging me on, but at *her*. More to the point, down at her. As in straight into her ample cleavage.

He glanced toward the court and waved at me, then shrugged as if to say, *What can I do?*

Tell her to go away, maybe?

Hot tears of anger blurred my sight as I turned back toward the net. He was talking to Melanie right there in front of me, during the second most important match of my season. How could Zach do this to me? Could he not stay away from her?

I glanced at Danielle. She pursed her lips in disgust. She couldn't seem to believe this was happening either.

Tanya tossed the ball and served.

All I could see was Melanie's curly hair bouncing as she

laughed. Her big blue eyes looking up at my boyfriend covetously . . .

The ball whizzed right by my racket.

"Forty, thirty!" the ref shouted.

My coach groaned. I glanced at the stands. Melanie was still over there, sipping water through a straw, making the simple act look somehow dirty. And Zach was utterly entranced.

"Come on, Bairstow! Get your head into the game!" Coach shouted.

Zach looked up then, as if startled to recall where he was. "Let's go, Noelle!" he shouted.

I narrowed my eyes at him. *Forget it. Just do this.*

I bounced into position and tried to look alive. Tanya reached up to serve.

Melanie giggled loudly.

The ball zoomed right for me. I reached for it, but it bounced off the rim of my racket and flew backward.

"Game! Set! Match! Zurich!" the ref shouted.

Dammit! I bent at the waist and gasped for breath, trying as hard as I could not to cry. I had never cried over losing a match, and I wouldn't let Tanya Zurich think she'd broken me down. Especially when these tears weren't remotely for her. I cleared my throat, straightened up, and went to shake her hand.

"Nice match," she said.

"You, too," I replied, my voice cracking.

Danielle barrelled way down the bleachers toward me. Coach marched over to give me her standard what-can-we-learn-from-this speech. But Zach was still talking to Melanie. He hadn't even realized that I lost.

Saturday night I sat at the kitchen table with my family and stared at my dinner plate, totally dazed. All I had done that day was lie around, watch TV, and nap on and off. I kept blurring my eyes in and out, making my mashed potatoes go fuzzy, then focused, then fuzzy, then focused.

In my mind I played yesterday's match with Tanya over again. If only I had won a few more points early on. If only I hadn't been so tired, maybe I could have put her away before Melanie ever got near Zach.

But I couldn't go back and fix it. I had to accept the fact that I had lost to a substandard player. That I had only won a four-seed for the tournament. Meanwhile Melanie had put away her two opponents with ease and was ranked number one. She had dominated two decent players and still had enough time to hook her talons into my boyfriend.

"Noelle, you should eat something," my mother said gently.

"I'm not hungry," I told her. My stomach constricted at the very thought.

"You look hungry," Faith said. "You look like death, in fact."

"Faith . . ." my dad scolded.

"Well, you do!" Faith said, ignoring him and ripping off a piece of her roll. "So you lost one match. Big deal. You'll kick ass at states. And, hey, this way no one will see you coming!"

I shoved my chair away from the table. I knew Faith was only trying to help, but I just couldn't listen to her optimism right then. "May I be excused?"

"Why?" my mother asked.

"I have to get ready for this party," I said. "Zach's picking me up in an hour."

"A party?" my father asked, pausing with his water glass halfway to his mouth. "Do you really think that's a good idea?"

"Actually, yeah. I think it's a great idea," I retorted.

"Noelle, don't take that sarcastic tone with your father," my mother stated flatly.

My mother is almost never stern, so I knew I was pushing it. I just wanted to get out of there.

"He's just worried about you," my mom added. "We all are."

"Maybe you should stay home tonight and get some rest," my father put in. "You do look a bit . . . " He didn't finish.

"I'm fine," I told them, trying to perk up. "Really. It was just a long week. But I think I need this party more than I need some rest."

Especially considering what happened the last time I blew off a party with Zach.

My family members exchanged wary looks. I sighed. I was so sick of everyone thinking they knew what was best for me. Couldn't they see I was trying to save a relationship over here?

"Look, if I don't feel well, I'll come right home. I

promise," I said. "I just . . . have to make an appearance."

"All right. If that's what you want," my father agreed finally. "But you're not getting up from this table until you eat something."

"Fine."

I picked up my roll and took a huge bite out of it. Instantly my stomach heaved, but I held my breath and managed to chew. The bread turned gummy and gross in my mouth, but I forced myself to swallow it. It got stuck halfway and I guzzled some water to help it get through.

"Better?" I asked my dad, my eyes stinging.

"Take that with you and finish it, and I'll feel even better," he answered.

I rolled my eyes at him but brought the roll with me when I got up from the table. As soon as I was upstairs, I tossed it into a wastebasket and went to get dressed.

This was an important night—Zach and I making our first appearance at a party together since our major public meltdown. I knew everyone was going to be watching us. The last thing I needed was to throw up in the middle of it. I'd eat tomorrow. When everything would finally feel normal again.

eleven

The seniors-only party was stifling, confined to the basement of Morris Robinson's house. Morris was one of the wealthier guys at school, so it was a *big* basement with a living area, a game room, and a laundry room . . . but it was still a basement. There were no windows, and about eighty people were packed in tightly, smoking, laughing, and being generally irksome.

None of this was good for a girl who hadn't eaten all day or slept all night. The moment Danielle, Jonah, Zach, and I arrived, I wanted to bail.

"Yo, Zach, Jonah! Wanna shoot some pool?" Zach's friend Luke shouted from the doorway to the game room. "We're playing for cash."

Zach and Jonah glanced at each other, then looked at

me and Danielle hopefully.

"Go ahead," Danielle said, shooing them along. "But if you win you gotta buy us something pretty."

I smiled as Zach kissed my cheek and jogged off with Jonah. Oddly, I felt relieved the moment he was gone.

"Let's get something to drink," Danielle said, pulling me toward the bar.

She mixed herself her favorite drink—a screwdriver "light on the screw"— then started to make me one.

"I'll just have the juice," I told her. I sat down on a chair that had just been vacated.

"Coming right up!"

Okay, this was better. The air was less smoky over here, and it seemed a little less loud when people weren't shouting directly into my ear.

"Here you go," Danielle said, dropping down next to me. She took a sip of her drink and smacked her lips. "Where's Aurora tonight?"

"I think Drake dragged her to that environmental rally at the college," I told her. "You know, Trent's thing?"

I wondered if I would have been there, too, if I had chosen Trent. It might have been nice to be out in the fresh air tonight instead of here.

"Are those two, like, *together* now?" Danielle asked, raising her eyebrows. "Because I'm sorry, but Drake is *weird*."

"I think they're just friends who're going to the prom together," I replied. "But who knows? Tomorrow she might call us up and tell us she's all in lo-o-ove."

"Yeah. She hasn't been in lo-o-ove in, like, a month. That's a long time for her." Danielle laughed. "So how about you? Are you all in lo-o-ove again?"

I forced a smile and sipped my juice. "Sure. Of course. Everything's great."

"Good. I'm glad to hear it," she said skeptically.

"What?" I asked, my stomach twisting.

"It's just, you don't seem happy," she told me. "You seem kind of blah, actually."

"Gee, thanks."

"No! I just mean—"

"Hey, Noelle?"

I looked up to find Tracy Walkow standing over me. She was more sober than she'd been at her own party, but she seemed kind of . . . concerned.

"What's up?" I asked her.

"You might want to come in here for a sec," she said. Her voice was flat.

My heart thumped with foreboding, and I pushed myself up from my seat. A major head rush threatened to take me right back down, and I pressed my hand to a wall to steady myself. Tracy was hanging by the door to the game room, waiting for me.

I walked over to her and looked across the room to the pool table. My entire stomach almost dropped right out of my body.

Melanie Faison was there, standing by the wall. What the hell? Was this girl *everywhere*? Or just everywhere Zach happened to be? As I watched, she took a sip of her drink

125

and handed Zach his pool cue. He thanked her and then bent to take his shot while she blatantly checked out his ass.

"What the hell is she doing here?" I hissed. "I thought this was a Jefferson party."

"Yeah. So did I," Tracy said.

"Noelle," Danielle whispered, touching my shoulder. "They're not doing anything. It's just a party."

"Please! She's practically stalking him!" I whispered back. From the corner of my eye I noticed a few people watching me and whispering. "What is up with this girl? Is she that freaking hard up, she has to keep coming after my boyfriend? Are there no eligible guys at her own school?"

"Maybe she can't get a guy at her own school," Danielle said uneasily. "I don't know. Maybe we should feel sorry for her."

"Please. That's about the last thing I'll ever feel toward her." I ducked behind the door and peeked back into the room. "And look at him! He's totally talking to her. Why doesn't he just tell her to back off already?"

"I don't know," Danielle replied with a nervous laugh. "Cuz he's polite?"

"Why are you always defending him?" I asked.

"I'm not! I'm just trying to make you feel better," Danielle said. "Calm down."

"I am calm," I told her, looking wildly around the living area. "He thinks it's okay to flirt while we're in a relationship? While I'm in the next *room*? Fine. I'll show him what *real* flirting is."

"What're you gonna do?" Tracy asked, scuttling up behind me.

My eyes fell on Derek Walton, the guy who had been crushing on me since Valentine's Day, if not longer. A jolt of exhilaration shot through me. All at once, I felt more awake than I had in days.

"I'm going to give my boyfriend a taste of his own medicine."

"You have the best legs in the entire senior class," Derek said to me, staring down at my bare knees as we sat on the couch. Derek turned out to be an even easier target than I'd predicted. He was already pretty drunk, so he had long since passed into uninhibited territory.

"You think?" I said, hooking one leg over his.

I blushed the second I did it, and Derek's brown eyes widened a bit. *Oops.* Maybe I had just taken this a tad too far. Of course, Melanie probably would have done that half an hour ago.

"Yo. Aren't you, like, with Zach still?" Derek asked me.

"Yeah, but that doesn't mean I can't talk to you, does it?" I asked him, tilting my head, not believing the sound of my own voice.

Derek smiled a toothy smile. "No. I guess not," he said. Then he burped right into my face. His breath smelled like jalapeño Doritos.

The things a girl has to do to wake up her boyfriend . . .

"Uh, Noelle? Can I talk to you for a second?" Danielle said, pushing through the crowd to stand in front of me.

"Actually, I'm kind of in the middle of something," I told her.

"I can see that," Danielle replied through her teeth. "It's kind of what I wanted to talk to you about."

"So talk." I was not getting up from that couch. I was not going to move until Zach came back from his epic billiards game and saw me. Until he felt that punch in the pit of his stomach that I felt every time I saw him with Melanie.

"Okay, are you *trying* to drive Zach right into Melanie's arms, or are you trying to get Derek's ass kicked?" Danielle demanded.

"Whoa, whoa. Who's kicking my ass?" Derek asked, his head lolling as he tried to focus on Danielle.

"No one," I assured him. "Danielle, just drop it, all right? I know what I'm doing."

"You know, I really don't think you do," Danielle said.

At that very moment Zach stepped into the room, laughing with Jonah. My instinct was to jump right off Derek, but I didn't move. Zach had to see this. He had to know how it felt. Finally Zach's gaze fell on me, and his entire expression changed. He looked as if he'd just had his heart torn out through his back. I can't say I wasn't gratified to see that he still cared.

"What the hell are you doing?" he shouted, crossing the room in two strides.

"Oh. Hi, Zach." I tried to sound casual, but in my nervousness I sounded shrill.

"Get off him, Noelle," he said, seizing me by the wrist.

I got up too quickly and stumbled a little, off balance. "What? We were just *talking*," I said pointedly. "What's the big deal?"

Zach ignored me. His chest heaved. His face was red with fury.

"Get up," he said to Derek.

"Why?" Derek asked.

"So I can beat the crap out of you," Zach replied, grabbing Derek's shirt.

My stomach clenched. Uh-oh. Honestly, in spite of Danielle's warning, I hadn't expected this to happen. I expected Zach to pick a fight with *me*, not innocent, drunken Derek.

"Zach, no!" I said, tugging his arm. "Leave him alone! It wasn't him!"

"What're you talking about?" Zach shouted. "He was all over you."

"No, he wasn't! I was all over him!" I shouted. Oh, God. Here it came. I was going to throw up. Again. Dammit. "I was . . . I was—"

There was no time. I put a hand over my stomach and staggered for the laundry room and the bathroom beyond. I was just able to get in there and slam the door behind me before it came. My whole body was racked with pain as I shuddered through it, and tears squeezed out the corners of my eyes.

"Noelle? Are you okay?" Zach asked, tapping lightly on the door.

"One second!" I shouted.

I pulled myself together. Then I wiped a hand roughly across my mouth and opened the door. Zach took one look at me and went pale.

"Are you all right?" he asked, stepping inside.

"No! No, I'm not all right!" I shouted. I let the tears stream down my face. I had totally lost control. There was no going back now.

"Calm down. What's the matter?" Zach asked quietly. He looked over his shoulder and closed the bathroom door behind him.

"You know what? Just do it already, okay?" I shouted at him. "If you want to hook up with Melanie again, do it! Get it over with! I can't take this anymore!"

If Zach wasn't as white as the linoleum before, he was now. "Who told you?" he asked.

I felt as if the entire room was crumbling around me. So he *had* hooked up with her. Then he'd fallen for the oldest trick in the book and admitted it. Hugging myself, I stepped back against the wall.

"No one told me," I said. "You just confirmed my suspicion."

For a split second Zach's eyes flashed with anger. He tipped his head back and knocked it against the closed door.

"Oh, my God. This is not happening," he said to the ceiling. Then he looked at me, his eyes pleading. "Noelle, it was just one time, okay? And it was while we were broken up. You have to believe me."

I stared at him icily. What better way to announce to

130

the world that you're lying than to say, "You have to believe me"? This was insane. If he was lying about this, then what else had he lied about? Had he been lying the entire time we were together?

"What about that night you were supposedly sick?" I asked him. "The night when you didn't answer any of my calls." He dropped his hands, and his face completely shut down. "Where were you that night? Tell me the truth."

"Noelle . . . "

"Zach, I swear . . . if you don't tell me the truth right now I'm never going to trust you again," I said.

Zach hung his head. He pushed his hands through his hair and blew out a sigh. "Fine. I was at a party," he said.

I gulped. "With her?"

"Yeah. It was a Washington party," he told me, driving a stake right through my heart. "But *nothing happened*," he added, his eyes begging. "We were just hanging out."

I covered my face with one hand and realized I was trembling. Of course I was trembling. I hadn't eaten or slept well in days, and the guy I loved was admitting that he'd spent time with another girl while we were together—and *lied* about it. I felt as if the last three years were flashing before my eyes. Had he been seeing other girls behind my back all along? How stupid was I?

"Noelle, I love you. You know that," Zach said, stepping toward me. The room was small enough that this one step put him mere inches away. I stared at the faded NASCAR logo on his T-shirt and saw the lines of his muscular chest through the fabric. I felt myself start to cave. I loved him, too, dammit. Why *did* I have to freakin' love him?

"No," I said, standing up straight. It was the only word I had the strength to shove out, but at least it was something. I couldn't let myself give in. Not this time. But I couldn't be this close to him either, or I *would* cave.

I started past him for the door, shoving him aside, but he grabbed me by the wrist.

"Don't go," he said.

"I have to," I told him. "I can't take this anymore. I can't take *you* anymore. Not right now."

"Noelle—"

"No, Zach. I have to . . . I have to think," I choked out, tears welling up all over again. "Please just let me go."

Zach sighed but finally released me. I fumbled for the doorknob and staggered out, hoping Danielle had never finished that drink of hers. Someone was driving me home from here this minute. And it definitely was not going to be Zach.

I stared at the glass of water and the plate of crackers on my bedside table. Every time my dad walked past the closed door of my room with his heavy gait, the water rippled. I blinked, and my eyes burned from staring blankly too long.

Outside the sun was shining, but barely a trace made it through my closed blinds and drawn curtains. According to the clock it was already after noon. I hadn't gotten out of bed all day. My mom and Faith had checked on me a few times—thus the crackers and water—but none of their chiding and wheedling could get me out of bed. Every time I lifted my head, every time I thought I'd found a comfortable position, I'd start to feel sick again. And every time I'd found something on TV or in a magazine to distract me, I was soon staring into space again, thinking about Zach.

"Who told you?" he'd said.

With that look of guilt. Of sickened, snagged guilt. What had he done with her? Did he kiss her neck the same way he kissed mine?

I squeezed my eyes shut tightly, my pillowcase bunched up in my fists.

I knew I couldn't blame Zach for anything he'd done while we were apart. After all, I'd shared those intense kisses with Trent. But if he'd been seeing her *before* we'd broken up, *before* our anniversary, then that whole special day with him was a sham. How could he say that it didn't mean anything? Whatever he'd done with her, it meant *everything*.

Downstairs, the doorbell rang, reverberating through the otherwise silent house. My heart flew up into my throat, and I sank down in the sheets. I could hear my mom talking and recognized the low tones of Zach's voice.

There was no way I wanted to see him. No way in hell.

My mother climbed the stairs to my room and knocked lightly on my door before entering. Thank God, she'd left Zach behind.

"Honey? Zach is here to see you," she said.

"Could you please tell him to go home?" I asked.

"Noelle, he looks upset," she said, taking a couple steps

into the room. "And he brought flowers," she whispered.

"I don't want them," I groaned, rolling over. "I can't deal with this right now, okay? Please just tell him I'm sick and I'll talk to him later."

"Okay, hon. I'll tell him," my mother said.

She closed the door behind her, and I took in my first real breath since the bell had rung. I heard the front door close, and finally my toes and fingers uncurled.

I was safe for now. I'd bought a little more time to figure out what I wanted to say. I just wished I knew how to *begin* to figure that out.

twelve

On Monday at lunchtime I didn't even bother going to the cafeteria. I'd done a stellar job of avoiding Zach all day, coming in slightly late and rushing from class to class, taking odd routes. Going to the cafeteria would obliterate all that hard work. Plus, I had zero appetite, and I didn't feel like listening to my friends as they tried to put a positive spin on what had happened. Instead I ducked into the library and took one of the private study carrels in the center of the room. I opened a textbook, crossed my arms over it, and put my head down, half on my hands, half on the cool, smooth pages.

A huge yawn racked my body. My eyes started to droop. Why was it that at night I lay wide awake staring at my canopy, but in the middle of the day I could fall asleep at the snap of my fingers? Why couldn't I just get back to normal?

A few minutes later my head jolted up with a start, and I realized I'd fallen asleep. I looked around, embarrassed. Luckily, there was no one in sight.

Then I heard a familiar voice and figured out why I had woken up so suddenly. Zach was nearby.

My heart started to pound. I held my breath. Ever so carefully I glanced around the side of my study carrel. Zach was standing in the hallway outside the double doors, talking to Tracy.

"I haven't seen her all day, and she's not at lunch," he said, looking upset.

"Well, maybe she stayed home," Tracy suggested with a shrug.

"No. Jonah saw her in English," he told her, rubbing his forehead. He leaned back against the wall. "She's avoiding me. I know she is."

"Why would she be avoiding you?" Tracy asked. "You guys just got back together, right?"

I sank back into my cubbyhole and pulled my legs up onto the chair. I couldn't believe I was hiding in the library. Hiding from *Zach*. How had my perfect relationship turned into a duck-and-cover mission? I hated that I'd made Zach look so worried, but even more I hated that *he'd* made *me* feel like *this*.

I rested my chin between my knees until I heard Zach and Tracy walk away. Then I finally relaxed. I just wished things could go back to the way they'd been before all this had started. When we'd been happy, and I knew exactly where I stood.

"Come on, Noelle! You've got to get that killer instinct back," Coach Carney said, clapping her hands as she patrolled the sideline at practice that afternoon. "Where's your serve?"

I wiped my brow with the back of one hand. Since I'd lost that match the week before, she seemed to feel the need to ride *me* and no one else. Just what I needed.

Across the court, Madison Jankow, an injured teammate, held the speed gun we shared with the baseball team. Last week I had been serving eighty-five miles an hour. My fastest today? Seventy.

I bounced the ball at my feet, trying to concentrate, but when I looked down, I saw two balls and four sneakers. I paused and closed my eyes for a second. The sun pounded down on my face. My temples throbbed.

Deep breath, Noelle, I told myself, sucking wind.

"Noelle! Are you okay?" Danielle asked from the next court.

"Fine," I heard myself say. But my voice sounded distant and fuzzy.

Come on. Just serve. Get Coach off your back.

I looked up, and my eyes crossed. There were two of Madison now, at opposite ends of my vision. My heart raced like an itty-bitty fist punching away instead of a full-sized heart. A heart that tiny couldn't possibly pump enough blood through a person my size. Something was wrong. Suddenly I couldn't breathe.

Come on, Noelle, focus. You're fine.

"Let's see that serve, Bairstow!" Coach shouted.

I'm not fine. I'm not, I'm not, I'm not.

I gasped for breath. Scared tears burned my eyes. My knees felt like jelly. I had to get control. I had to.

"Noelle?" Danielle said. She sounded as panicked as I felt.

On autopilot, I lifted my racket. I squinted and tried to focus, but Madison was just a double blur now. I tossed the ball into the air, looked up at the sky, and everything went black.

Before I opened my eyes, I heard my mother's hushed voice. Somewhere something was beeping. A voice on a speaker overhead called for assistance in room four-fourteen. Where was I?

I opened my mouth, and it was dry and gummy. A cough escaped my throat, and my head throbbed with pain. When I opened my eyes, all I saw was a dimly lit room and a window of vertical blinds. I groaned and lifted my hands to my face. There was a twinge in my left arm, and I put it down again.

"Noelle?"

"Mom?"

I felt her cool hand on my face and relaxed slightly. The pain in my head receded into a dull ache. Still painful but not deadly.

I blinked, opened my eyes, and looked at her. She

smiled, but her forehead was lined with concern.

"You're awake!" she said happily.

"How do you feel?" a handsome doctor in scrubs and a white coat asked me. He had sandy brown hair and crinkles around his eyes when he smiled.

"My head hurts," I said, touching my temple with my right hand this time. There was something stuck to my skin. I felt around. It was a circular sticker with a wire attached. "What's that?"

"It's a monitor," he said, lifting my wrist to take my pulse. "We're trying to determine why you fainted."

"Fainted?" I echoed, thoroughly confused.

My mother had moved to the end of my bed. "On the tennis court," she confirmed. "Do you remember anything?"

I tried, but it was all fuzzy. For some reason all I could see was Madison Jankow and a tennis ball. I took a breath and coughed again.

"May I have some water?" I asked.

"Sure, honey," my mom said, practically pouncing on a plastic pitcher next to my bed.

My bed. In the hospital. Suddenly, far too late, it occurred to me that I was actually *in a hospital*. With an IV in my arm and a monitor attached to my head. This could not be good. Instantly my pulse started to race.

"Am I going to be okay?" I asked.

The doctor looked at a beeping machine next to my bed, then smiled at me kindly. "Take a deep breath. You're going to be fine. I'm Dr. Levine, Noelle. Do you mind if I do a few tests?"

"No," I said.

He asked me a bunch of questions, like what day it was and who was president of the United States. Then he had me follow his finger with my eyes and made a note on his clipboard. After that he checked my ears and nose and throat and listened to my chest while I slowly breathed in and out.

When he was done, my mom handed me a cup of water, and I sipped it. It felt cool and comforting as it ran down my throat and right into my empty stomach. Suddenly I realized that for the first time in days I didn't feel nauseated. You'd think that the shock of waking up in a hospital would make me sick, but I felt fine. Aside from the fear and the headache.

"Noelle, I have a few questions for you, if you don't mind," the doctor said. "They're kind of personal. I can ask your mom to leave if you want me to. It's up to you."

I glanced at my mom. She looked so worried, and somehow the last thing I wanted was to be left alone just then.

"It's okay. She can stay."

My mother smiled and sat down on the side of my bed. She took my hand and held it.

"Okay, first of all, have you been eating regularly lately?" he asked.

My heart skipped, and I shot a furtive peek at my mother. She stared back with a no-nonsense look in her eyes. I guessed there would be no evading this question now.

"Not really," I said, squirming.

"What does that mean, exactly?" he asked. "Two meals a day? One?"

I felt like an idiot. Here he was concerned that I might be eating only one meal a day, when in actuality it was even less than that.

"One," I said. "Sometimes."

He raised his eyebrows, his pen poised above the clipboard. "Sometimes? What did you have to eat today?"

My face heated up as he and my mother watched me closely.

"It's okay, honey," my mother said softly. "Just tell the truth."

"Water?" I said. "And half a granola bar."

My mother pressed her lips together and the doctor made a note.

"Is this a normal intake for you on a regular day?" he asked.

"No," I replied. "Not really. It's just that when I'm stressed out, I can't eat. I get sick to my stomach."

"So you don't avoid food on purpose," he said, sounding almost relieved.

"No. Only when I know for sure I won't be able to keep it down," I told him.

He made a note. My mom patted my hand.

"How about sleeping? Have you been sleeping the last few nights?"

"Not really," I admitted.

He made another note.

"Noelle, may I ask what has you so stressed out?" he asked me. "Your mother tells me you're an overachiever. Straight As, valedictorian, ace tennis player. Do you feel a lot of pressure to maintain these standards?"

"No," I answered instantly.

"Noelle . . . " my mother said.

"I don't, Mom," I said. I wiped my sweating palms on the bed's waffle blanket. "Honestly. I know how this is gonna sound, but that stuff isn't really that hard for me."

"Then do you know why you've been feeling all this stress?" my mother asked. "Where's it coming from, Noelle?"

My heart twisted, and I sank down a bit in the bed. I didn't want to answer that question. Not even to myself.

The doctor exchanged a look with my mom. He took a step closer to my bed.

"You don't have to answer that right now, Noelle," he said. "But it's important for your health that you deal with it. Because whatever it is, it's taking a toll on your body. And a girl your age with so many opportunities and her whole life in front of her shouldn't be in a hospital bed. She should be out with her friends living her life and having fun."

I nodded, tears welling up in my eyes. "I know."

He glanced at my mother, and she stood to follow him out.

"I'll be right back," she told me, squeezing my arm. "Okay."

The moment they were out in the hall, tears slipped from

my eyes and streamed down my cheeks. I couldn't avoid it forever. I knew exactly what was stressing me out. It was Zach. Zach and Melanie. Zach and whether or not I could trust him.

My relationship had put me in the hospital. How could I have let this happen? I was usually so cautious and in tune with myself, but I had entirely missed the biggest problem in my life. The guy I loved had become bad for my health.

The next afternoon, I had just settled in on my parents' comfy couch with a cozy blanket and remote in hand, when the doorbell rang. Dr. Levine had released me earlier in the day with a firm directive to take care of myself, which I had every intention of doing. I got up and opened the front door to find a huge vase of roses, camouflaging the deliveryman. My breath caught when I recognized Zach's sneakers below the blooms.

"Hey, Noelle," he said, placing the flowers on the coffee table, next to a few other offerings.

"Hey," I said, retreating back to the couch.

He shuffled over, looking both concerned and completely awkward. Then he shoved his hands into the pockets of his varsity jacket.

"May I?" he asked, leaning toward me.

"Sure, I guess," I said.

He kissed my forehead, which almost made me cry, then perched on the edge of the couch.

"Noelle, what happened?" he asked. "Are you okay? I

mean, I freaked out when Danielle called me."

"I'm fine," I said. "I'm gonna be fine."

"Thank God." He blew out a sigh, and reached over, taking one of my hands in both of his. "If there's anything I can do. I mean anything . . ."

I took a deep breath and glanced away for a second. I knew what I had to do, but now that he was here, concerned and holding my hand, I didn't know how I was going to do it.

You fainted, Noelle. In front of the whole team. What if that had happened while you were driving or when you were alone?

I needed to deal with this. It was doctor's orders. I leaned forward and looked at him. He stared back at me hopefully with those hazel eyes of his.

"Zach," I began, clutching the blanket at my side. "I think we need to . . . break up."

"What?" he blurted. "Noelle, come on. I want to help you get better."

"That will help me get better," I said.

He blinked. "I don't get it."

"I haven't been eating or sleeping," I told him. "And it's because of you. And Melanie."

Zach swallowed hard. "Noelle, I'll never see her again. I have zero feelings for her, I swear. It was just all one big, stupid mistake. I'll never be in the same room with her again if that's what you want."

Wow. He really wasn't going to make this easy for me. He was sincere. He didn't care about her. He cared about me.

But that didn't change what he had done. It didn't

change the fact that I was never going to trust him again. And as long as that was true, I wouldn't be able to take care of myself.

"That's sweet, Zach," I told him. "But I need to be alone for a while. I have to . . . concentrate on getting better," I said, borrowing a few words from another speech Dr. Levine had given me.

"You want to be alone?" Zach repeated.

"Yeah," I said.

"But . . . what about the prom?" he asked.

I smiled wanly. "You can have our tickets," I told him. "I'm sure you'll have no problem finding a date."

Even as I said it, my heart broke at the thought of his going without me. I really hoped I was doing the right thing here. I hoped my cute doctor knew his stuff. He had said to cut the stress out of my life, and Zach was the source of my stress.

"Noelle—"

Just then Aurora and Danielle burst through the door without knocking, carrying a ton of balloons and gift bags. They hesitated for a split second when they saw Zach, but then Aurora rushed to the couch and threw herself at me.

"You're okay!" she said, kissing my cheek. Her skin was warm, and I nearly burst into tears again at the weird scent of lavender that always surrounded her. "You really scared the crap out of us, you know?"

I smiled as she leaned back.

"Everything okay in here?" Danielle asked tentatively, holding the balloons.

"No. It's not," Zach said.

"Actually, it is." I felt a bit more firm with my friends there. "Zach, you should probably go," I told him. "Thanks for the flowers."

"But, Noelle—"

"Zach, I can't talk about this anymore," I interrupted. I knew it was cruel, but I didn't know how else to get him to leave. And I needed him to leave. "Please, just go."

Aurora and Danielle looked at each other, and Zach stared at me a moment longer.

This had to be over. It was for my own good.

"Fine," he said finally. He stood and looked at me, shifting his weight from foot to foot. "Can I at least call you to see if you're okay?"

I swallowed and nodded. "Just give me a couple of days."

"Okay," he said. He glanced at Danielle and Aurora, then left.

I leaned back into the couch pillows, relieved. All the muscles in my body relaxed more completely than they had in weeks. I hadn't even realized how tense they'd become in the first place, I was so used to the feeling.

"Are you okay?" Aurora asked, climbing onto the couch to sit next to me. She put an arm around my shoulders, and instantly I started to cry.

"Not really," I choked.

"But you will be, right?" Danielle said, joining us.

"Yeah. I will be," I said.

And it was the truth. Because even though I had just broken up with my boyfriend of three years, I felt free—and more at ease than I had in quite a while. As Aurora cuddled into me and Danielle flipped the TV to an ancient episode of *Friends*, I knew I had done the right thing. Zach was officially part of my past. Now I just had to concentrate on moving forward. I had to concentrate on me.

The End

The Choice Redux

Well, Zach was definitely not the one for me in the end. Want to try again and help me find a new love? Flip back to page 99 and choose someone else!

You Chose Trent

nine

I slipped out of Mrs. Lane's room and ran down the hall to the back stairwell, then jogged upstairs to meet Trent before he got to his history class. The moment I stepped into the hallway, he stepped up out of the front stairwell.

It felt like fate.

"How did you get here so fast?" he asked, his face lighting up when he saw me. We walked toward each other to meet right in the center of the hall. I could practically hear the movie music swelling in the background. "Is your headache gone already?"

"Actually, yeah," I said with a smile. I'd never really had a headache, but I *was* feeling monumentally better now that I had finally made my decision. "Trent, I have something to ask you."

"What's that?"

"Would you like to go to the senior prom with me?" I said, tilting my head slightly.

Trent smiled. A huge, happy smile. It sent my heart twirling and whirling.

"Definitely," he said. "I would be honored to be your date to your prom."

I laughed at his formality—and from my giddiness. "Thank you, kind sir," I joked. "Now, if you will excuse me, I must depart for class."

Trent chuckled as I turned around. Then he grabbed me by the hand and spun me right back toward him. "Hang on a sec," he said.

My breath caught as he leaned in to kiss me. Right there in the middle of the hallway. About two seconds in I had to force myself to pull away, or I would have melted in front of dozens of classmates and never lived it down.

"I'll see you later," he said, taking a step back.

I didn't move. Mostly because I knew it would take another minute before my legs started working again. "Absolutely. See you later."

I had definitely made the right choice. A girl couldn't give up kisses like that. At least, not a sane girl.

"What a totally gorgeous day!" Aurora said, stepping out of my car in the parking lot on Wednesday morning.

"It's almost a travesty to be in school," I agreed.

I pushed the door's lock and slammed it shut. The sweet morning breeze lifted my hair off my back. The sun warmed my face. A tingle of pleasure rushed over my bare arms.

"Look at you! You're loving life, aren't you?" Aurora said as we started across the parking lot.

"Why not? I made my decision, I have a date for the prom, and it's a beautiful morning," I said, a skip in my step. "And it's a perfect day for tennis."

"True. I must come to your match this afternoon and catch some rays," she said.

"I thought you were all about skin protection," I reminded her.

"I am! But I need a *little* color before the prom," she told me. "Otherwise I'm just going to disappear in my dress."

She had a point. Her mother had given her the beautiful, retro, strapless dress that she'd worn to *her* prom, but it was cream colored, almost the exact same tone of Aurora's skin. She was going to need at least a slight tan to pull it off.

"Oh, hey! There's your boyfriend!" Aurora teased as we approached the front door.

A ton of people were hanging out on the steps around the trees that fronted the school. Trent was over by a large oak with his usual posse. One of them strummed a guitar while the others talked. Trent was wearing a heather-gray T-shirt with a tree logo on the front, and a pair of baggy brown cords. He looked as adorable as ever.

"He's not my *boyfriend*," I told Aurora, stifling a smile.

"Yet," she whispered. She raised her eyebrows as she approached the group.

"Ha-ha," I said.

The question was, did I want Trent to be my boyfriend? Was I ready for another commitment already? The corpse of my relationship with Zach was barely cold. Maybe I should keep my options open a bit . . .

But then, what would really change? We were already going to the prom together. Trent kissed me almost every time he saw me. We held hands all the time. We just hadn't said the *b* and *g* words to each other yet. Maybe it was about time to make it official.

I stopped next to Trent and slipped my hand into his. He grinned at me and kissed my cheek.

Yeah. This felt good. It felt right. Why shouldn't he be my boyfriend?

"Hey. I have a question for you," I said.

"What's up?" Trent asked, his blue eyes soulful.

"Do you want to come to my match this afternoon?" I asked him. "It's not a huge one, but I'd love it if you came to see me play."

Zach had almost never missed one of my matches. Boyfriends came to see their girlfriends play all the time.

Trent grinned. "I'd love that, too!" he said. "Yes, definitely. I'll be there."

He wrapped an arm around my shoulders and gave me a squeeze. Behind him Aurora flashed me a teasing thumbs-up, winking elaborately.

I laughed and turned away. Aurora had hooked me up. Just like she always did, whether it was with RingPops or boys. The girl was good to have around.

* * *

"Forty-love," the ref announced. "Match point!"

I pumped a fist and turned toward the bleachers as I walked back to serve. For the ten millionth time I scanned the faces in the crowd. A few parents and a couple of friends had shown for the match, but there was still no sign of Trent. Where was he? I was one point away from being done for the day.

"Come on, Noelle! Put this one away!" Coach Carney barked, clapping her hands.

I glanced at Aurora, who sat at the top of the bleachers. She shrugged and then pointedly looked to her right. I followed her gaze and nearly tripped. Zach was there, standing near the end of the benches, his arms crossed over his chest. He didn't look too happy.

"Great," I muttered under my breath, stopping at the back of the court. Just what I needed. I had been avoiding Zach all week. Why did he have to pick a match to finally corner me?

Don't let it get to you, I told myself. *You were going to have to deal with him eventually.*

I took a deep breath and shut out my surroundings—Coach Carney, my teammates, the crowd, even Zach, faded away. None of it mattered. It was focus time.

I reached up and served.

Cora Richter, my opponent, grunted as she ran to make the shot. She returned it, but her shot was clearly wide. I didn't even make a move. The ball landed a foot out of bounds.

"Yes!" Aurora shouted.

"Game! Set! Match! Bairstow!" the ref announced.

I grinned. After that loss to Melanie the week before, I had to admit it was nice to be back on the winning side of things.

I glanced at the stands one last time. Trent was nowhere in sight. Ugh. The relief faded. Was it wrong that I wanted Zach to see some other guy supporting me?

Why *wasn't* he here to support me?

I strolled to the net to shake Cora's hand, then walked to the fence, where Zach was waiting. I had a feeling this was not going to be pretty.

"Hey," Zach said, pushing his hands into the front pockets of his jeans.

"Hey," I replied. I avoided direct eye contact by shoving my racket into its bag and zipping it up.

"So, I heard you were going to the prom with that sop," he said coolly.

I looked up at his derisive tone. Two seconds in his presence and I was already fed up. "Well, if you already heard it, then why are you even here?" I asked.

"Nice," he said angrily. "I come over to your house and pour my heart out to you, and you treat me like crap."

I sighed, and my shoulders slumped. "I'm sorry," I told him. "I was going to tell you."

"When? When I showed up at your front door with a corsage?"

"Zach, I never said I was going with you," I reminded him. "I'm sorry, but I decided to move on, okay? You should, too."

Zach smirked. "Don't worry. I will."

"I wasn't worried," I snapped back. This was so not the way I wanted to end things between us—snippy and mean—but if he wanted to be immature, there wasn't much I could do about it.

"See ya 'round," Zach said flatly. Then he turned and stalked away.

It was amazing how quickly things could change.

"You all right?" Aurora asked, jumping down from the bleachers.

"Fine," I said, shouldering my bag. "Great, in fact. I am *so* glad I stuck with Trent."

I just wished I knew where he was.

That night I sat on my bed and drew my phone into my lap. I hadn't heard from Trent all afternoon. Every second I was expecting a phone call of apology, or at least an explanation, but nothing. Looked like I was going to have to call him.

Normally my pride might have stopped me from doing this, but I was actually kind of worried about him. He had been so psyched about coming to the match, I felt something might have happened. So part of my motivation was to make sure he was all right.

I held my breath, picked up the phone, and dialed.

"Hey, Noelle!" Trent said when he picked up on the first ring.

He sounded fine. Happy as always. No hint of apology or dread in his voice. It was just . . . Trent.

157

"Hi," I said, confused.

There was a moment of silence.

"What's up?" he said finally.

"Oh . . . uh . . . " Right. I had called him. I got up and paced around my room. "Hey, I was just wondering . . . what happened to you this afternoon?"

"This afternoon?" Trent asked blankly.

What the heck was going on here? Was this a joke?

"Yeah, you know . . . my match?" I said, pausing in front of my desk.

Another moment of silence. Then a huge intake of breath.

"Oh, my God! Noelle! I'm so sorry!" I imagined him slapping a hand to his forehead. "I spaced. I just spaced."

I sat back on the surface of my desk, bummed. Okay, so I'd gotten my apology, but I was also offended. He spaced? I had reached out and asked him to come watch me play—one of the most important things in my life—and he'd spaced?

"At lunch Jamie Lindquist and I decided to call a special Save Our Planet meeting this afternoon to make signs for that rally at the college next weekend," he said quickly. "Everyone was so excited, and I got caught up, and I guess I forgot . . . I'm really sorry."

"Oh," I said. Well, at least he hadn't just forgotten for no reason and gone home to watch TV or something. "That's okay."

"Are you sure? I don't want you to be mad at me," he said openly. "I mean it. I messed up."

I smiled. Could he be any sweeter? "It's fine," I replied,

and I meant it, too. After all, one of the things I liked about Trent was how much he cared about the environment and his other causes. I wasn't going to make him feel guilty for skipping one easy match of mine to help save the world.

"So, did you win?" he asked.

"Yep," I said, dropping down onto my bed again and making the throw pillows bounce.

"Good. Congratulations," he said. "I wish I had seen it. I really do."

"I know. Don't worry about it," I told him. "How did the sign making go?" I settled in against my headboard for a long chat, crossing my legs at the ankles. I was proud of myself for not whining to him and also happy to have a boyfriend who cared about something other than himself. If he even *was* my boyfriend. But I supposed that was something we could figure out later.

ten

"It's gonna be so much fun," Danielle said as we approached my locker on Friday after school. "Morris said he's having Jefferson seniors only. Totally exclusive."

"Cool," I said, starting on my lock. "Can't wait."

The truth was, I couldn't focus that much on tomorrow night's party. In about ten minutes Danielle and I would both be on the bus to Crestwood High for the county tournament, which would determine our ranking for the state championships. Melanie would be there, too—and even though I probably wouldn't be playing her, I had to get myself psyched up. The girl couldn't resist trash-talking every time she saw me. All I wanted was to have some comebacks ready and to win a higher seed than she did.

"You're going, right?" Danielle said, flicking something

from underneath one of her long fingernails. "I mean, you're not going to let this whole Zach thing keep you from partying. It is your senior year."

"No. I'll be there," I replied, grabbing my tennis bag out of my locker. "I promise."

By tomorrow night this round-robin tournament would be over and I would be more than ready to kick back.

"Hey, Noelle!"

We both looked up to see Trent loping down the hall toward us. His blond hair was a bit tamer than usual, and he'd also added a couple new colors to his rubber bracelet collection.

"Hi, Danielle," he said, just before laying a quick kiss on my lips. A quick kiss that, nevertheless, tossed all thoughts of Melanie and tennis right out of my head. "Just wanted to wish you luck."

"Thanks," I told him, giving him a little squeeze.

Trent leaned back against the locker next to mine and fished a piece of gum out of one of the many pockets in his cargo pants. "So, what were you ladies talking about? Tennis strategy?"

"Please. We don't need strategy," Danielle said with mock cockiness, tossing her hair over one shoulder. "We will beat all comers, for we are the mighty Jefferson High Patriots."

"I like your attitude," Trent replied as he popped the gum into his mouth.

I laughed. "Actually, we were talking about this party

that Morris Robinson is throwing tomorrow night," I said. "Hey! Do you want to come with?"

It wasn't as if I was actually nervous about attending a party that Zach would be at, but how cool would it be to walk in there with my brand-new almost-boyfriend?

"Noelle, I told you. It's seniors only," Danielle said pointedly. Then she smiled at Trent. "No offense."

"None taken. You guys were juniors a few months ago, too, you know." He blew a bubble. "Anyway, we can't go, Noelle. We already have other plans."

I blinked as I slammed my locker. "We do?"

"Yeah. Tomorrow night's the rally at the college, remember?"

My heart completely dropped. How had I spaced on the rally? It was pretty much the only thing Trent talked about.

"What? Noelle, you cannot miss this party," Danielle began.

I bit my lip and looked from Trent to Danielle and back again. Trent and an environmental rally or Danielle and one serious party. I knew which way I was naturally leaning—toward Danielle and enjoying the end-of-the-year festivities. But I *had* told Trent I would go with him, like, two weeks ago.

"Come on, Noelle. You can go to a party anytime," Trent said, taking my hands and giving me a cute little pout. "This is for a good cause."

Did he really have to look at me, all pleading eyes, like that?

"So's the party!" Danielle yelled.

Trent slipped an arm around my shoulders and faced Danielle. It was as if he already knew I was going to cave. "Really? What cause is that?" he asked.

"The Noelle Deserves to Have Some Fun Foundation," Danielle announced, her expression defiant.

"The rally will be fun!" Trent countered. "They're having this guitar trio all the way from Milwaukee."

"Oh, well, then, I submit," Danielle said sarcastically. "I mean . . . *Milwaukee*. We all know that's the epicenter of fresh music."

I laughed and took a deep breath. "Danielle, I'm sorry, but I told Trent I'd do this with him a while ago."

"Come on! You've gotta be kidding me! This is a seniors-only party! Everyone's gonna be there."

I looked up at Trent. "Not everyone."

Trent smiled and kissed me, and I beamed.

Danielle threw her hands up and groaned. "Fine. I'll meet you at the bus. I gotta go get my stuff," she said, walking off.

I felt bad, but I knew Danielle would forgive me. It wasn't as if she'd be going to the party alone. She always had Jonah. And as much as I wanted to go to Morris's and chill, I also wanted to be there for Trent. Clearly it meant a lot to him, so I was willing to compromise. Wasn't that what people in relationships did for each other? Compromise?

However, before I got to either the rally or the party, I had to get through a Saturday afternoon of working with Ryan—who I hadn't seen since our kiss.

* * *

"Can I get a black-and-white cookie over here?" Ryan called out on Saturday afternoon with none of his usual playfulness.

"Sure."

I opened the pastry case and plucked out a cookie with the metal tongs. All I could feel was my pulse pounding in every inch of my body—which it did pretty much every time Ryan acknowledged my existence these days. Neither one of us had mentioned the kiss since it happened, and the longer we avoided it, the more awkward the whole thing became. At this point it was almost like there was a hot-air balloon called "The Kiss" filling the entire coffeehouse and using up all the oxygen.

"Thanks," Ryan said.

He didn't even make eye contact as he took the plate and handed it to his customer. I couldn't stop stealing glances at him. Under his apron he wore a formfitting white T-shirt and a brown suede studded belt holding up his perfectly faded jeans. I might have chosen Trent, but Ryan was still the hottest guy I knew.

I still could not believe he wasn't gay—

Stop it, Noelle. So he's hot. Big deal. You chose Trent. Now you have to concentrate on getting your friendship back on track so that you don't have to dread coming into work all the time.

Ryan slammed the register closed, and I took a deep breath. Sun poured in through the front windows, and every time the door opened there was a burst of sweetly scented, warm spring air. We should have been in good moods. We should have been chatting and laughing and making our shift fly by. Instead, the clock was dragging.

All right. Just say *something!* I told myself.

"So . . . have any big plans for tonight?" I asked finally.

"I have this gig in the city with my band," Ryan mumbled, leaning back against the counter and crossing his arms over his stomach. He looked at the floor, not at me. "A preliminary audition for this competition. It's kind of a big thing."

"Really? How so?" I asked.

Ryan shook his head. "I don't really want to talk about it, actually."

My heart twisted in my chest. "Ryan—"

"I just don't want to jinx it," he said, grabbing a plastic cup and rolling it between his palms. "What about you? Anything going on this weekend?" He finally looked at me, and his green eyes seemed almost hopeful. What he was hoping for, I had no idea.

"Actually . . . I'm gonna be on campus tonight," I told him. "I'm going to this environmental rally with Trent."

Ryan's face went slack. "No, you're not," he said incredulously.

I blinked. *Sorry?*

"Yeah, I am," I said, confused.

"Come on! That crap?" Ryan said vehemently, tossing the plastic cup onto the counter.

Whoa. Step back. What was with the sudden anger here? One second I barely exist, and the next I'm being attacked?

"What do you mean, 'that crap'?" I shot back.

"Noelle, those people have no idea what they're talking about," Ryan said, suddenly sounding much older. "The state wants to build low-income housing on that land they're trying to 'save.'"

"Really?" I said. I wrinkled my nose. Why hadn't Trent mentioned this?

"Yeah. It's not like we're gonna let some corporation come in to build an office complex or something. We're trying to help people," Ryan told me. "Plus, the acreage was decimated by a forest fire a couple of years ago. The groupies keep talking about all the wildlife, but all the wildlife fled a long time ago and never came back. It's uninhabitable."

"Come on," I chided. "How is that possible? Why would all these people be freaking out?"

"Because they don't bother to listen," Ryan said adamantly. "They don't do their research or care about the facts. They just hear that some parkland is going to be sold off, and they start a crusade."

I turned around and hoisted myself up to sit on the back counter, my hands pressed down on the Formica surface at my sides. "Are you sure?" I asked him uneasily. "I mean, how do you know all this?"

Ryan scoffed. "Because unlike this Trent kid, I pay attention."

"Don't be mean," I told him.

Ryan's jaw clenched. "I'm sorry. It's just . . . this is all anyone at school has been talking about. And I think people should get their facts straight, that's all."

"Well, maybe *you* don't have all the facts," I replied, shrugging. "Maybe . . . maybe in a couple years all the wildlife *will* come back."

"Yeah, and in the meantime hundreds of needy families will be living on the streets so that the land can be there when Thumper returns," Ryan said flatly.

Okay. He had a point.

"Look, Noelle, everyone's entitled to an opinion," he said, his tone softening. "I just know you, and . . . I know you'd want to hear all sides before putting yourself on the line for a cause."

I smiled. There was definitely a compliment in there somewhere. "Thanks," I said.

"No problem," he replied grudgingly. The front door opened, and a gossiping gaggle of middle-aged women walked in. "I got this," Ryan said, tossing a towel over his shoulder. "Good afternoon, ladies! What can I get you?" he asked.

I laughed as the women reacted to the gorgeousness before them, one of them even blushing at the very sight of him. Part of me felt ten times better. It looked as if there was still a chance for our friendship. But another part of me was completely unnerved.

Why hadn't Trent ever mentioned this low-income housing thing? Did he even know about it? Did he know all the facts about the cause he was so adamant about? Or did he just not care?

* * *

"I feel very super-spy right now," Danielle said, glancing up from her computer monitor at Mr. McSwiggen, our computer lab teacher.

"Just tell me if he's coming my way," I said.

I had minimized the window I was *supposed* to be working on so that I could search the Web for information on Trent's rally. Ever since my conversation with Ryan I had been dying to find out which one of these guys was right—but when I'd gotten home from work, I'd been too exhausted to even turn on my computer. This was my first chance.

"Ah. Here we go," I whispered.

Google had come up with several articles on the subject, mostly from local papers. I opened the first one and started to scan it.

"I don't believe this," I said.

"What?" Danielle asked out one side of her mouth. She clicked her mouse a few times and kept her eye on the pacing McSwiggen.

"It's right here in the second paragraph," I said. "'Local officials had hoped to utilize the land for a low-income housing project that would provide homes for hundreds of citizens, but the development has been put on hold as environmental lobbyists dispute the plan.'"

"Ha! I knew that Trent kid was up to no good."

"It's not that he's up to no good," I corrected her. "I mean, he has a good cause, too. Right?"

"Personally I'd rather see needy families getting homes than let some dead trees rot in peace," Danielle replied.

I sighed and opened the other articles. Almost every one of them mentioned the potential benefits of the housing project. How could Trent not tell me about this?

"McSwiggen alert," Danielle mumbled.

My heart skipped a beat, and I maximized my work window. McSwiggen gave me a sour look as he strolled by, but he kept walking. I let out a breath.

"So. What're you going to do?" Danielle asked me.

I thought of Trent's earnest face and of how excited he was about the rally. The last thing I wanted to do was disappoint him.

"Maybe I should just go with him and hear his side," I suggested. "Maybe I'm missing something."

"That's very sensible of you," Danielle said with a nod.

"Thanks," I replied.

I just hoped it turned out that Trent and his friends were doing the sensible thing, too. Otherwise this could get mighty confusing.

"How amazing is this?" Trent asked, taking me by the hand as we navigated the crowd that had gathered on the great lawn on campus. He was wearing a homemade SAVE THE FOREST T-shirt and gripping a rolled up tube of flyers in his free hand. "Look at all these people! Corey and Tag really got the word out!"

"Corey and Tag?" I shouted to be heard over some random chanting that was going on around me—then ducked as a soft Frisbee whizzed by.

"They're the people we met last time we were here,"

Trent told me, glancing over his shoulder. "They're so dedicated to their cause. I could definitely learn a lot from them."

Yeah? Like the fact that this whole campaign of yours might be totally bogus?

"Uh, Trent? Could I talk to you for a second?" I asked as we emerged into a small open space.

"Sure." He stood on tiptoe to scan the crowd, taking it all in.

"Trent! Over here!" I waved a hand in front of his face.

"Sorry," he said. He shook his head and turned his attention to me, which had to be difficult, considering the mayhem around us. On a covered stage at the top of the lawn some girl was shouting about cruelty to animals, while off to my left a group of chicks in flowered skirts danced around in a circle. "What's up?"

"Listen, have you heard anything about what the state wants to *do* with the land?" I asked.

Trent scoffed. "No. But I'm sure they want to throw up another Home Depot or something. Which, by the way, no one needs."

My forehead wrinkled. He knew what he was rallying for, but he had no idea what he was rallying *against*.

"Actually, they want to put up low-income housing," I told him. "They want to get needy families off the streets and out of the rundown areas of the city."

"Really?" Trent said vaguely, looking around again. "I didn't hear anything about that. It's probably just propaganda, you know? Some crap they made up to silence us."

"And we will not be silenced!" some shirtless dude shouted, overhearing us.

"We will not be silenced!" Trent called out in return.

Everyone around us clapped and cheered.

I flushed and grabbed Trent's hand. "Don't you think you should know all the facts before getting behind a cause?" I whispered through my teeth. "I mean, you might be keeping a bunch of worthy families from having homes!"

Trent looked at me blankly for a moment as if trying to process that. Seconds later he smiled. Apparently he had rejected my argument before the processing was complete.

"Come on, Noelle! It's fine! We're doing something good here," he said, slipping an arm over my shoulders and turning me around with him. "Look at all these people! Why would they all be here if it wasn't a good cause?"

I looked into Trent's wide blue eyes, at his optimistic smile, and suddenly realized something that I couldn't believe I had missed all along. Trent was a follower. A "true believer." He was into his cause, yeah, but even more than that, he *enjoyed* being part of something. Even if he wasn't entirely certain what that something was.

I looked away. Clearly I was not going to get through to him. He wasn't going to hear anything he didn't want to hear. But I brushed it off—relationships are about compromise. This was his thing, and we still had my thing coming up, which reminded me it was time for a change of subject anyway.

"So, listen, I wanted to talk to you about the prom," I

said, leading him toward a huge oak tree. "Danielle's going to host the pre-party so we can take pictures and everything, and Jonah priced out the limo, but if you want to go with Aurora and Drake, we can talk about that."

Trent tore his eyes away from the action long enough to wince. "Actually, the prom is June eighth, right?"

"Yeah . . . ?"

"Yeah, I've been meaning to tell you . . . I'm not gonna make it."

The Earth suddenly stopped rotating. A group of kids playing hacky sack nearby cracked up laughing. It felt as if they were laughing at me.

"What?" I said, shocked.

"Yeah, there's gonna be this campout in Springfield that night, and I need to be there," Trent told me. "We have to have our voices heard, Noelle." He picked up one of my hands and laced his fingers through mine, apparently not noticing that I was now stiff and cold. "I was actually kind of hoping you'd come with me."

I laughed. It was an automatic reaction. And it sounded almost like a bark.

Trent leaned back and looked at me, confused. "What?" he said.

"You're seriously asking me to skip my senior prom to go camp out in the state capital?" I asked.

Trent's brow creased. "Yeah. You can go to a dance anytime, Noelle. We're talking about saving the world."

I stared at him, and suddenly everything became perfectly clear. Trent and I were not meant to be together. He was a sweet guy, but if he thought he could just offhandedly dismiss my senior prom—a night I'd been waiting for my entire life—then he didn't know me at all. And he definitely didn't see the world the same way I did. I mean, calling the senior prom just another dance you could go to anytime? Was he nuts?

"Save the forest! Save the forest! Save the forest!" a group of kids around us began chanting, pumping their fists in the air.

It was like a wake-up call. I looked around at all the unfamiliar faces, some painted with little flowers, others pierced in places no sane person should ever be pierced. I felt as if I was coming out of a deep sleep. What was I doing here? This wasn't me. I was no activist—at least not for *this* cause. If Trent was a follower, what did that make me? I had been trailing around behind him just like he was trailing around behind these people. This wasn't a relationship compromise, it was me giving in to what he wanted. I was completely losing myself.

It was about time I did something I wanted to do.

"Trent, I'm sorry, but I have to go," I told him, standing up straight.

"What?"

"And, to be honest, I don't really think we should see each other anymore," I added.

His face completely fell. "What?" he repeated, letting go of my hand.

"Look, you're a really nice guy, but I don't think we're compatible, you know?" I said. I was so ready to escape and be free that I wasn't even feeling all that nervous. I just had to get these words out so I could leave.

Trent squeezed his rolled tube of fluorescent-colored flyers with both hands. "I . . . I guess I can see that."

"I mean, you want to be here, and, if I'm being really honest about it . . . I don't," I said with a shrug.

He nodded, his eyes on me. "I see. Well, if that's how you really feel . . . "

"I do."

"Okay. If you're not feeling it then you shouldn't stick with it," he said. "You've gotta be true to yourself, right?"

I smiled. He was still very cute. Someday he was going to make some wide-eyed hippie girl a perfect boyfriend.

"Thanks for understanding," I told him, leaning forward to kiss him on the cheek.

"No problem," he replied. He looked confused, but I had a feeling he'd get over it once that guitar trio from Milwaukee took the stage.

"I should go," I said. "Do you think you can get a ride home?"

Trent smiled and spread his arms as if to encompass the crowd. "Hey, I'm surrounded by a thousand of my closest friends."

You go, nut-ball, I thought, and almost laughed. But I controlled myself. "Okay. Have fun!" I told him. Then I gave him a hug and got the heck out of there as fast as I possibly could.

eleven

In the car, I cranked up the radio and started laughing as I glanced at the campus gates in my rearview mirror. I was free! Completely and totally free. I was going to that party to find Danielle and have a good time. Yes, Noelle Bairstow was ready to let loose.

I took a deep breath and shook my head. I couldn't believe how silly I'd been for the past couple of weeks. I mean, Trent Davis as my boyfriend? What was I thinking? One pair of gorgeous eyes and a few knee-melting kisses and I was lobotomized. I thought *he* was the perfect guy for me? Please. Maybe he was book-smart and cared about things, but what did we have in common? *Nada.* Zip. Zilch.

Apparently rebound goggles really existed. And mine had been a seriously strong prescription.

I turned onto the ramp to the highway and hit the gas. The moment I did, my car lurched. My stomach flew into my throat as every single light on the dashboard was suddenly illuminated. Then the engine died. Just like that. My car slowed, and the guy in the Jeep behind me slammed on his brakes and leaned on his horn.

Just think. Get off the road, a little voice in my mind said calmly.

Somehow I wrestled control of myself and eased my still-rolling car off the roadway and onto the shoulder. The Jeep peeled out behind me, kicking up dust in its wake. I sank down in my seat, trying to catch my breath. I put the car into park and stared at all those blinking lights.

What the hell had happened? The lights said I was out of gas, oil, and coolant. That I had to check the engine. That I had to check the brakes. Was it possible that every single part of my car had malfunctioned at the exact same moment?

I turned the key to off and back on, but absolutely nothing happened. The car was dead.

Great. I was stranded in the middle of a highway ramp, fifteen miles from home. What was I supposed to do?

I grabbed my bag off the passenger seat and fished out my cell phone. I was about to dial home when I realized my parents were out for the night at some hospital benefit. Instead, I dialed Faith's cell.

It rang once, twice.

"Come on . . . pick up," I said through my teeth.

Finally the line connected, and my heart leaped.

"I'm ignoring you. Leave a message."

Great. Voice mail.

"Faith! My car just died in the middle of nowhere. If you get this message, call me back right away," I said.

I hung up, frustrated. Outside, car after car was breezing by. Couldn't they see I needed help over here? Where was a cop when you needed one?

I dialed Danielle but got her voice mail, too. Shocker. She was at one of the biggest parties of the year. She probably couldn't hear her phone.

Next up, Aurora.

"Noelle?" she shouted. There was a ton of noise in the background.

"Thank God! Aurora! Where are you?"

"I'm at the rally!" she shouted. "Where are you?"

"You're at the rally? At the college?!" I shouted back.

Sure enough, I heard the chant: "Save the forest! Save the forest!"

"Yeah! Wait! I can barely hear you! Where are you? Are you here somewhere? Me and Drake have been looking all over."

"Aurora! Listen! I just left, and my car broke down!"

"What?"

I nearly exploded from frustration. "My car! I'm in my car and it broke down. Can you come get me!?"

"What!? Noelle, I can't hear you! The concert is starting!" Aurora yelled.

"Aurora! I need help!" I shouted.

"Noelle! I can't hear you! Sorry! Maybe we'll—"

I hung up. That was pointless. I groaned and leaned forward, bumping my head on the steering wheel. I was going to be here all night. It was getting darker by the second, and I was starting to get scared.

Okay, there has to be someone else you can call, I told myself, gripping my phone. *Zach?*

I snorted. I'd rather get kidnapped than call him for help. He'd never let me live it down.

I took a deep breath and looked at my phone. There was only one other option. One other person I trusted. The problem was, I wasn't entirely sure he would want to help me.

But I had no choice.

I found his name in my contacts list and pressed SEND. I closed my eyes and said a quick prayer for mercy as the phone rang.

He picked up on the third ring. "Hello?"

I held my breath.

"Ryan? It's Noelle. I'm kind of stuck. . . . "

I leaned back against the passenger side of Ryan's car while he talked with the tow-truck guy, making sure they were both clear on what was wrong and what their plan was. It had taken Ryan less than half an hour to get there, and when he showed up he was actually out of breath from concern. I wanted to throw myself into his arms and hug him in thanks, but, considering our recent history, that didn't seem like the wisest idea.

I watched as he and the tow-truck guy finished talking,

and my insides felt all warm and almost nervous. Ryan was wearing a tee that clung perfectly to his body and brought out the gray flecks in his eyes. My hero in fraying cotton.

Finally they shook hands, and the tow truck growled to life. I stood up straight as Ryan walked to my side.

"He's going to take it to that garage near your house," he told me. "He said it was the timing belt."

"What's a timing belt?" I asked.

"I have no idea," Ryan admitted with a shrug and a laugh. He opened the car door for me. "Let's just hope that mine is in working order."

I smirked and sat down in his passenger seat. Ryan's car was an old, battered clunker with torn seats and a cinnamon-scented air freshener dangling from the rearview mirror. When he got in on the other side and slammed the door, the whole car shook.

"Doesn't instill confidence," I joked.

"Rosanna's a good girl," he said, patting the dashboard. "She'll get you where you need to go."

"You named your car Rosanna?" I asked.

"Every good car needs a name. That way they never turn on you," he said.

"Yeah, right."

Ryan looked at me, raising one eyebrow. "Ever name your car?"

"No," I said.

"Case closed," he replied.

I laughed, and he started up the engine. The wail of a

guitar solo blared from all speakers and scared the crap out of me. I actually yelped.

"Sorry," he said, turning down the volume. "Hate it when that happens."

That was when I remembered what he was supposed to be doing that night. "Oh, my God. Your audition. You're missing your big audition."

"It's not a huge deal," he said.

"No! Ryan, it is! You even said it was! God, I'm *so* sorry."

"It's okay," Ryan said as he pulled into traffic. "It's not like I was going to leave you stranded. Besides, they don't need a drummer."

"Funny," I said. "The drummer is only the most important part of any band."

Ryan glanced at me, surprised. "You think so?"

"What? You keep the beat. Everyone knows that."

He smiled, and I blushed.

"I hope they're not mad at you," I added. "Were they mad?"

"Don't worry about it," he said. "Really. Let's talk about something else. So, what happened tonight? Rally didn't do it for you?"

I sighed and, with much chagrin, laid out the whole story for Ryan. "Turns out you were right," I finished. "Trent actually had no idea what he was talking about. I'm such an idiot."

"You're not an idiot," Ryan said immediately. He pulled off at our exit and stopped at the bottom of the ramp. "You just made the classic rebound relationship mistake."

"Yeah? What's that?" I asked.

"Well, you're heartbroken, so you go out with the first guy who asks you, and then you get all invested." He turned onto Main Street. "You start making all these compromises just because you're used to being with someone and you don't want to mess it up. Because you're afraid of being alone."

My face reddened even more. He had hit several nails directly on their heads. "Sounds like you've been there before."

"Oh, I have," he said. "And it was not pretty."

"You never told me you had a serious relationship and a rebound," I said, feeling a little miffed.

"Apparently I never even told you I was straight, so we have some catching up to do."

We both laughed. That was when I knew for sure that everything was going to be okay between us.

"Which house is yours?" he asked.

"That one. With the brick on bottom and the white on top," I said, pointing.

"Anyway, you should never compromise," Ryan added, rolling to a stop. He put the car into park and turned to face me, his hands on his thighs. "You're too good for compromise."

My heart thumped extra hard. If anyone had told me that I would have ended this night alone in a car with Ryan Corcoran, staring at his luscious lips, I would have laughed myself silly. But there he was. And everything was fine.

More than fine, actually. He wasn't mad at me for choosing Trent. In fact, he was looking at me as if all he could think about right then was kissing me.

I knew the feeling.

And suddenly I knew what I had to do.

"Ryan? Would you go to the prom with me?" I blurted out.

Slowly Ryan smiled. "Sure you're not just rebounding from your rebound?" he asked.

"I'm sure," I told him, pulse racing. "This is going to sound crazy, considering, but I've kind of had a crush on you forever."

"Really?" he said, trying not to smile back. "Well, that works out because I've kind of had a crush on you forever."

With that Ryan leaned in and gently touched his lips to mine, sending a series of delicious shudders throughout my body. During our first kiss I'd been in complete shock, but this time I kissed him back. I put my arms around his strong shoulders, touched the skin of his arms.

I felt all of it, and it all felt so, *so* good. It made me forget every other kiss I'd ever experienced.

Ryan was stunning in his tux. So stunning that every girl at the prom gaped every time he walked by. There we were, at our senior prom in this gilded country club on Lake Michigan, with a view of the boats on the water, and no one could take their eyes off my date. Not even me. While I waited near the windows overlooking the shore, I watched him walk off to the dry bar and felt nearly drunk with attraction. He should wear a tux every day. Seriously.

"Gay, huh?" Zach said, sidling up to me and staring Ryan down from across the room.

I glanced up at my ex. He wasn't looking too shabby himself. Of course the fact that he had brought Melanie Faison to our prom in that slutty minidress of hers made him a lot less attractive.

"What can I say?" I said. "I turned him."

Zach looked at me and smiled weakly. "Why do I actually believe that?" he said.

I blushed. "Because you know how very sexy I am," I joked back.

Zach looked as if he was about to say something meaningful. My breath caught. Did I want to hear this? No. Not really. I had no interest in anything mushy or nostalgic that Zach might have to say. The only guy at this prom that I wanted to hear sweet somethings from was Ryan.

"Zach! This is my favorite song!" Melanie announced, running over, boobs bouncing everywhere, and grabbing his hand. "Let's go dance," she said, shooting me an irritated look.

"Okay," Zach said, downing the rest of his drink. "See you, Noelle. Have fun."

"You, too," I told him, feeling very mature.

As Ryan started his walk back through the ballroom, I noticed a group of girls whispering and laughing nearby. Suddenly Aurora raced over to me, arriving at the exact same moment as Ryan. She looked pale, even though she had gotten that tan she had hoped for.

"What's the matter?" I asked.

"You're never going to believe this!" she gasped, putting a hand to her chest in her typical dramatic fashion. "All the Save Our Planet kids were just arrested in Springfield. Something about disturbing the peace! Dana Tarkjian got there late and saw them getting hauled off! She just called Drake on his cell!"

"Are you kidding?" My jaw dropped.

I imagined Trent being shoved into a cop car in hand-cuffs. Was he okay? Was he scared? What was he going to do?

"I bet that Trent kid is wishing he had come to the prom with you right about now," Ryan said, handing me a bubbling glass of Sprite.

"Seriously," Aurora agreed.

I couldn't help but smile, an image of Trent in a jail cell full of environmentalists popping into my mind. I pictured him still making impassioned speeches, shouting at the guards, and going on about the cause. Why did I get the feeling that Trent was actually just fine? That maybe he'd wanted to get in trouble.

"Aren't you worried?" Aurora asked.

I rolled my eyes. "Actually, no. Trent is probably *glad* he was arrested."

"What?" Aurora said.

"Aurora! It means his voice was *heard*!" I said right-eously.

They both laughed. I took a sip of my drink before putting it down and dragging Ryan toward the dance floor. Trent was out there doing exactly what he wanted to do, and now it was my turn. And, as far as I was concerned, it was way past time to party.

The End

The Choice Redux

Well, that kind of worked out. But not exactly as planned. Think I can do better on the next try? Go back to page 99 and pick again.

You Chose Ryan

nine

After practice that afternoon I went directly to the Magic Bean. I knew Ryan was working, and now that I had my prom tickets, I was dying to see his face. Dying to get another chance at that kiss so I could actually kiss him back. The last time I had completely frozen up in shock.

That was *not* going to happen again.

I walked in right behind Tracy Walkow and Donna Dumakis. They were so engrossed in their conversation, they didn't see me, which was good. The last thing I wanted to do right now was get sucked into a wrist-corsage versus pin-on debate. I had bigger things on my mind.

"What? Like he's not gonna get me a corsage at all?" Donna was saying with a laugh. "He'd better."

I stepped around them and saw Ryan standing behind

the counter chatting with Mitch. One look at him and I almost melted. I couldn't believe that after all this time I actually had a shot with Ryan Corcoran. If he still wanted me, of course. That kiss had been days ago already. What if he regretted it?

Why would he regret it, moron? He *kissed* you, *remember?* I had to get a grip.

I snuck up from behind, so Ryan blocked Mitch's view of me.

"Thank God I'm out of high school," Ryan muttered to Mitch under his breath, glancing toward Donna and Tracy. "I hated all that superficial crap."

My heart slammed into my shoes.

"Please. I didn't even go to my prom," Mitch said.

"Me either. No interest," Ryan replied. "It was probably so lame."

He picked up a bottle of water from the counter and turned around, lifting it toward his mouth. He stopped in his tracks when he saw me standing there. I must have looked stunned, because realization overcame his face, and he blushed.

"Noelle," he said, lowering the water bottle.

Oh, God. I couldn't believe I had been seconds away from asking him to my prom. How stupid was I? He was in college. He was in a band. Couldn't I have figured out that he would have "no interest" in going with me? That he would think it was "so lame"?

At least I had stopped myself in time. If I had asked him and he had laughed in my face, I might have crumbled.

192

"Hi," I said casually. I felt sick to my stomach. I grabbed his water bottle from him and chugged half of it down.

"I'm sorry. I didn't mean to make fun of your prom," he said quickly. "I know you're probably going, and—"

"Nice one, genius," Mitch sang behind him.

"Don't worry about it," I said, waving him off. "Proms *can* be totally lame."

Ryan looked a bit confused but managed to smile. "Yeah. So . . . what're you doing here?" he asked. "You're not on the schedule."

Right. Good point. What was I going to do now?

"I know. I just . . . listen, I . . . I wanted to ask you something," I said, my stomach twisting into nervous knots.

"What's that?" Ryan asked. He smoothed his hair back with both hands, then crossed his arms over his chest. Totally smooth, confident, and sexy. How was it possible he actually wanted *me*?

Tracy and Donna finally approached the register. Mitch shoved us aside and went to help them, clearly sensing there was a matter of great importance going on over here.

"Uh, I wanted to see if you wanted to go out with me sometime," I said in a rush. "To—I don't know—dinner or something?"

My voice squeaked on the last word. I'd never asked out a guy before. I held my breath and waited.

"Yeah?" Ryan asked. His entire face lit up.

"Yeah," I said, feeling as if I might collapse.

"Definitely," he replied with a huge nod. "All right. Definitely."

I had to laugh. Never in my life had I been so glad to have been completely misled about something. Ryan was not gay. We were going to go out on a date. I was going on a date with this beautiful, older, artistic, sweet guy.

Life could not be any better.

Trent was hanging out with his usual posse—all of them wearing serious expressions and even more serious message T-shirts—before the first bell the following morning. I took a deep breath as Aurora and I approached him from the parking lot. It was a totally gorgeous spring day, and the lawn was packed with people enjoying the sun as long as possible before getting cooped up in class all day. I, however, could not revel in the weather, knowing what I was about to do.

"Just let him down easy," Aurora whispered to me as a light breeze tossed her short hair around.

"What do you think I'm gonna do? Go over there and tear his head off? I actually like the guy," I told her.

"Then why are you doing this again?" she asked, eyebrows raised.

"Uh, hello? Ryan Corcoran?" I said.

"Oh, right. Say no more! Girl's gotta do what a girl's gotta do." She glanced at Trent, who grinned the moment he saw me. "But I do not have to watch," she added, distressed. She patted me on the shoulder for strength, then rushed inside, her long skirt swishing behind her.

"Traitor," I muttered under my breath. I walked up to Trent, and he kissed me quickly on the cheek.

"Good morning!" he said, slipping an arm around me.

Could he lay on the guilt any thicker? Not that he knew he was doing it. I glanced around at his friends, who were chatting while another guy strummed his guitar.

"Trent? Could I talk to you for a sec?" I said, tilting my head. "Over here?"

"Sure," he said, completely clueless. "Be right back, you guys."

I walked toward the trees that lined the front path and paused. Trent smiled at me. I took a deep breath and ignored the nervous pounding of my heart. Better to get this over with. After all, I was going to have to do it a second time today. No need to drag out the drama.

"So, listen, I don't think this is going to work out," I told him.

Trent's eyes narrowed. "What?"

"This," I said, staring at him. "Us."

He lifted his head slightly, surprised. "Oh."

"I just . . . don't think we're that compatible," I told him. "You're all into your causes and old movies and everything, and I'm . . . not."

"Oh. Right," Trent said, blinking a few times as he took this in. He stared past me for a moment, then looked me in the eye. "Well, that's okay. It's actually probably better."

"Better?" I asked.

Maybe I was breaking up with him, but was it wrong that his comment kind of offended me? Where was the heartbreak here? *You're the one who didn't want drama,* a little voice in my head reminded me.

"Yeah. I have a lot going on right now with the forest rally coming up and everything," Trent told me. "I should probably focus on that. And, hey, if you don't feel it, you don't feel it, right?"

Oh, I'd felt it. Every time I kissed him I'd felt it. But that wasn't enough to base a relationship on.

"Thanks for understanding," I said with a smile.

"No problem," he said. "I guess I should get back to my friends."

"Yeah," I said.

"Yeah."

He nodded once, then turned and loped off. I took a deep breath and blew it out. One down, one to—

"You broke up with him."

Oh, crap.

I turned around to find Zach standing right behind me, a cocky grin on his face. He stared at me knowingly, triumphantly.

"So, we're going to the prom," he stated.

I swallowed. *Oh, man.* This was not going to be pretty.

"Actually . . . " I said, wincing.

Zach's eyebrows came together, but the smile didn't falter. The idea of rejection was *that* foreign to him.

"Zach, I don't think we should get back together," I told him softly.

"What? But you just dumped the sop," he said, gesturing at Trent and his friends over my shoulder.

"Shh! Don't call him that!" I said through my teeth. Luckily Trent was too engrossed in conversation to notice.

Zach huffed a sigh. "Noelle, I don't understand. Why did you break up with him if we're not getting back together?"

Because that guy you were paranoid about who I told you was gay is not gay, and I think he might actually be the most perfect guy on earth?

Yeah. That would go over well.

"Because," I said, struggling for words. "Because he's not right for me either."

Zach stared at me. "Oh. So I'm not right for you all of a sudden."

My guts twisted at the hurt in his voice, but I couldn't backtrack now. I'd made a decision, and I had to stick to it. "I'm sorry, Zach," I said honestly.

"Fine." His hazel eyes darkened, full of betrayal and shock as he backed away. "Have a nice . . . whatever." He turned and stalked off.

I watched him go and felt a flicker of uncertainty in my stomach. Had I really just said no to Zach? The supposed love of my life?

God, I hoped I was doing the right thing.

But then I thought of Ryan and instantly, automatically, smiled. I trusted Ryan. I knew that he would never hurt me—at least not on purpose. Whatever the future held with Ryan, it had to be better than constantly arguing with Zach and feeling suspicious of him and Melanie.

I had to concentrate on myself right now. And that meant concentrating on Ryan.

✳   ✳   ✳

A couple of nights later I was studying at my desk when my cell phone rang. I checked the caller ID, and when I saw Ryan's number, my pulse raced. I grinned giddily and picked up.

"Hey," I said, leaning back in my chair.

"Hi there."

It was still so cool just to hear his voice on the other end of the line—something that never used to happen unless he was calling about work. I glanced out the window at the full moon in the sky and sighed as my heart pitter-pattered away. So this was what a relationship felt like at the beginning—warm and fuzzy and exciting and nervous. I had forgotten all about it.

"What're you up to?" I asked.

"Not much. Listen, we said we were going to go out this Saturday, right?" he asked tentatively.

Something about his tone made my spirits droop, and I sat up a bit straighter. My fingers clutched the phone.

"Yeah?"

"Crap. That's what I thought," he said under his breath. In the background I heard a guitar wail and the screech of feedback.

"What's going on?" I asked, my throat suddenly dry.

"Me and the guys just found out we made the semi-finals for the Showdown," he said quickly. His voice dropped, and I could tell he was trying not to be overheard.

"The Showdown?" I asked.

"Yeah. It's this competition they hold every year in the city," Ryan told me. A door closed, and suddenly the background noise was gone. "It's kind of a big deal. Actually, it's a huge deal. Whoever wins is guaranteed a contract with a record label."

"That's amazing! Ryan, that's really *so* great," I said, trying my best to sound enthused. In fact, my heart was pretty much coughing and sputtering. "So, you want to cancel?"

"No!" Ryan said vehemently—so vehemently I almost jumped.

"No?"

"No. Definitely not. Do you know how long I've been waiting to go out with you?" he asked.

Now I was full-on grinning. I was glad he couldn't see me. "Okay, so . . . "

"So what do you think about coming into Chicago with me and the band?" he suggested. "You can watch the show, and then we'll—I don't know—grab a late-night snack or coffee or something. And then, hey! Maybe I can come to one of your matches next week."

"One of my matches?" I asked.

"Yeah. I've been kind of wondering why you've never invited me to one. I'd love to see you in action."

Okay. Now I was dizzy. How perfect *was* this guy?

"Right. We'll have to, uh, do that. Your gig, I mean. And coffee. Cuz we currently don't drink enough coffee," I joked.

"Good point. Ice cream. We'll get ice cream. Or pie!" he exclaimed.

He really *was* psyched to go on a date with me.

"I don't care. We can get whatever," I said with a laugh.

"So you'll come?" he asked.

"Absolutely. Hey! It'll be the first time I see you play!" I said.

"Sweet. It has definitely been too long," he replied. "So I'll pick you up at seven or so?"

"Sounds good," I said.

We hung up, and I sat back in my chair, feeling completely content. A concert and a late-night something-or-other in the city? It sounded better than good. It sounded amazing.

I spun around on my chair and faced my closet door. Now for the details. What, exactly, did the date of the drummer in the band wear to his gig? I was drawing a total blank.

"Faith!" I shouted. "I need you!"

This was a decision that called for reinforcements.

ten

Ryan was hot. Ridiculously, scorching hot. Behind his drum set, under the stage lights, he was an actual rock star. He pounded away, cocking his head back and forth to the beat, sometimes closing his eyes to feel the music. I could not take my eyes off him. He wore a black T-shirt and jeans with a knit cap holding his longish hair close to his head. The ring on his thumb flashed in the crazy stage lights whenever he went for the cymbal. A little sweat shone on his brow. I memorized every detail.

"Uh-oh! Someone's hypnotized!"

I looked up to find Marie Something-or-Other, the girlfriend of the lead singer, Brody Walsh, sitting down across the table from me with a fresh drink.

"I think I am!" I shouted back with a laugh.

Marie was the leader of the groupies—a pack of kids from Ryan's school who never missed a show. She had cocoa skin and long, long hair that tumbled down her back in tiny curls. She wore a tank top with the band's name—Lazy Daze—BeDazzled on the front. And yes, even with a semi-cheezy BeDazzled tank, she was the most gorgeous girl in the club.

The dark, loud stuffy room was jam-packed with people who had sardined themselves into old, unbalanced chairs around water-ring-stained tables. The air was thick with smoke and the scent of beer, making it hard to breathe without an oxygen mask. At least they were letting in under twenty-ones. Unfortunately, those of us who *were* under twenty-one had to wear this garish pink bracelet thing to let the waitresses know we were soda-only people.

"They're so good!" I shouted at her as I toyed with the tight band around my wrist.

"I know!" Marie yelled back. "You should have come to one of these things sooner. You've really been missing out."

She wasn't wrong. The members of Lazy Daze were insanely talented. Their music was of the emo/punk variety, and each song was tighter than the last. I could definitely imagine hearing them on the radio.

The song ended, and the entire place went nuts. I stood up and cheered, glancing at the record company peeps in the back of the club. This was only a preliminary round of the Showdown, but apparently they had come out to check the crowd reaction to each band. I wanted to give them exactly what they were looking for.

Ryan grinned, took a sip of his water, and winked at me. I sighed and sat back down. My date was a rock star. Period.

"I just can't believe Ryan's actually dating a high schooler," Jeannie, a girl to my left, said as I settled in.

"Jeannie!" Marie scolded.

"No offense," Jeannie said offhandedly, flicking her dark hair briefly out of her face before hunkering down and letting it fall forward again.

"None taken," I answered with false sweetness.

"So, what time does he have to get you home?" Jeannie asked. "Do you have to be in bed before *SNL*?"

"Jeannie, shh!" Marie hissed again.

I turned my face away.

"What? I'm just saying. It's not like she can hang," Jeannie said. "You probably have Girl Scouts in the morning, right?"

Something inside of me snapped, and I imagined what Danielle and Aurora would say if they were sitting there.

"Are you in love with Ryan or something?" I asked point-blank as Lazy Daze launched into another song.

Marie's jaw dropped open, and she looked at Lea, another girl at the table. Jeannie turned beet-red. She stared at me with narrowed eyes.

Catfight! Catfight! my mind chanted as my adrenaline started to rush.

"Whatever," she said finally, then turned and hid behind her hair again.

I glanced at Marie, feeling triumphant.

"*Nice one,*" she mouthed, impressed.

I was pretty impressed myself.

"How did you guys meet?" Lea asked, sucking her pink drink through a straw. She was a cute redhead with a zillion freckles and had a bit of a ditzy vibe going.

"Actually, we work together," I told her, shouting again to be heard over the music. "We've known each other for months, but we just sort of got together last week."

"Omigod! That's you? You're the girl from the coffeeshop!" Lea exclaimed happily. "Omigod! He's been talking about you *all year*! Hasn't he?" she asked, looking around.

"He has," Marie concurred, smiling at me.

I had no idea what to say to that, and my skin was rapidly overheating, so I simply grinned and returned my attention to the stage. I couldn't believe it. Ryan really *had* been waiting a long time to go out on a date with me. He'd even told his friends about me. I took a deep breath and relaxed. I could get used to this.

"You guys were unbelievable!" I gushed.

Ryan paused in front of a little dessert place called Sweet Thang and opened the door for me.

"You think?"

"Are you kidding? They *loved* you. I loved you." I nearly tripped over the threshold when I realized what I had just said. "I mean the band. I loved the band."

Ryan laughed. "Don't worry. I get it."

Embarrassed, I averted my eyes from his and looked around. The restaurant was humming with activity.

Couples and small groups huddled around tiny black tables with steaming cups of coffee and big hunks of delicious-looking cakes. Music played overhead, and I heard the familiar sound of a hissing cappuccino machine.

It was still fairly early in the evening. While the rest of Lazy Daze and their friends had stuck around to see the competition play, Ryan had given up the opportunity to hang with me so that we could have our date. Considering how shocked his bandmates had been at his desertion, I knew he normally would have stayed. I was still sort of reeling over the fact that he'd bailed to spend time alone with me.

"Well, it was pretty much our best set ever," Ryan said. His face was flushed from the exercise and the excitement. If possible, he was even better looking than usual.

"What can I get for you?" the lady behind the counter asked with a slight French accent.

"Noelle?" Ryan asked.

I placed my order—opting for carrot cake and coffee—and Ryan got tiramisu and espresso. He paid for our desserts as I checked out a few of the more sophisticated-looking couples all around us, putting a sweetly romantic cap on their evenings. I realized with a start that we were doing that, too. Ryan and I. Out on a romantic date. Who knew?

"Go ahead and find a seat. One of our waitresses will bring over your order," the counter person said with a smile, handing Ryan his receipt.

"Thanks." He slipped his wallet into his back pocket

and looked around. "Come on. Those people by the window are leaving."

"How did you find this place?" I asked as I followed him across the café.

"I did some research," Ryan told me casually. "I figured since I messed up our first date before it even started, I'd better find someplace cool to make it up to you."

My face flushed. He'd done research. "Please. You did not mess up our night," I said as I slid onto the red velvet banquette. "Watching you play was . . . "

Mesmerizing? Transcendent? A complete and total turn-on?

"What?" Ryan said.

"It was just incredible."

Ryan beamed. "Glad you liked it. It really was the tightest gig we've had in a while," he told me. "And I have you to thank for it."

I glanced at him, and he looked at me tentatively, almost embarrassed.

"What do you mean?" I asked.

"You're gonna think I'm insane," Ryan said, rubbing his forehead and closing his eyes.

"Tell me," I prodded.

He turned on the couch slightly and looked at me. His green eyes were laughing, just begging me not to mock him.

"Well, I think I played better with you there," he said.

"Come on," I replied, instantly blushing.

"No! I'm serious! Just seeing you in the audience . . . it

was like . . . I don't know . . . like a whole other level of adrenaline," he told me. "I could do no wrong."

"Wow." What was I supposed to say to that? I was so flattered, I was drawing a complete blank. "Well, okay, then. You *are* insane."

"Thanks. I appreciate that."

We both laughed as the waitress came to deliver our orders.

"So, listen, there's something I wanted to ask you," I said tentatively.

"Go for it," Ryan said.

"It doesn't bother you that I'm in high school, does it?" I began once the waitress was gone.

"What?" Ryan seemed legitimately surprised. "No. Why would it?"

"I don't know. . . . The other day you said you were so glad to be out of there, and then Jeannie kind of thought it was weird—"

"First of all, I'm glad to be out of high school because my particular high school sucked," Ryan said. "Secondly, ignore Jeannie. That girl is prematurely bitter."

I snorted a laugh, then slapped a hand over my mouth.

"Besides, who cares what year of school we're in?" he asked. "How old are you anyway?"

"Eighteen," I replied, grinning.

"So am I," he said.

I couldn't have been more baffled if someone had just driven an EL train right through the restaurant.

"No. You're not," I said.

"I don't turn nineteen until the end of August," he told me.

"Shut up!" My mind reeled. Was anything I had thought about Ryan actually true?

"What? Is that a problem?" he teased.

"No! It's just . . . all this time I thought you were this older, more sophisticated—"

"And *gay*," Ryan said pointedly.

"Exactly! And *gay* guy," I said with a laugh. "And now I find out you're really just this lame, straight, *young* person."

"Lame, straight, and young, huh?" Ryan said, kicking back and crooking his arms behind his head. "Yeah. That's pretty accurate."

I laughed again. Never in my life would I have thought that a first date could be this good, this relaxed, this fun. But it made perfect sense. Ryan and I already knew each other so well, there was none of that getting-to-know-you awkwardness. It was as if we'd been dating for months, and we *knew* we liked each other, but there were still so many exciting firsts to come.

"So, how late can you stay out?" Ryan asked me as we headed back toward the 'burbs in his clunky car.

"I don't technically have a curfew," I told him. "But if I were to get home, say, after midnight, my dad might have a coronary."

"So we have an hour before we put your dad in the hospital," Ryan said, glancing at the clock.

"Basically," I replied, watching the highway lights fly past.

"Do you want to come back to my dorm and hang out for a little while?" he asked.

I felt as if a hot, white spotlight had just been flicked on over my head. Go back to his dorm room? To do what, exactly?

"Are you sure we have enough time?" I asked.

"I think so. It'd be cool for you to see where I live," he added. "I mean, unless you want to go home . . . "

"No. That's fine," I told him, not wanting to look like a prude. Besides, this was Ryan. I trusted him, right?

"Good. Because I don't want to take you home yet," Ryan said with a completely innocent and non-lascivious smile as he took the exit for the college.

Sigh. He just didn't want the night to end. And I was right there with him. So we'd hang in his dorm room for half an hour, and then he'd drive me home. Case closed. Unlike a certain other someone I knew who felt the need to turn every date into a game of "How Far Can I Get Tonight?"

Still, as we approached his room, my legs were shaking. From behind various closed doors came the sounds of pounding music, parties, and general mayhem. This was *college.* And maybe Ryan wasn't technically older than me, but he was *so* gorgeous. He could probably get anything he wanted from any girl on this campus. I mean, all kinds of things went on at college that didn't necessarily go on in my world.

"Is your roommate home?" I asked hopefully, as Ryan fished out his keys.

"I have a single, remember? You know that," Ryan said.

Oh. Right. Damn. I *did* know that. A single. All the better to seduce you with, my dear.

Ryan stuck a key into the lock and turned it. I felt as if my heart was making its way to my mouth.

"Wait!" I said.

Ryan jumped. "What?" he asked, startled.

"I . . . I'm not going to have sex with you," I said, rather shrilly.

All the color drained out of Ryan's face. "Uh . . . okay. I wasn't really expecting you to."

Suddenly I felt like a grade-schooler with a serious naïveté problem. What was *wrong* with me?

"Oh," I said.

"I was just thinking we could hang out," he said. He shrugged. "Maybe *make out*. A little," he added in a whisper, sending an excited shiver right through me. "Did you really think I just wanted to bring you here to have sex?"

I rolled my eyes and looked at the floor. "I'm sorry. I just . . . you're older, and—"

"No, I'm not," Ryan reminded me with a grin.

I smirked. "And you're *so* cute."

"No, I'm not," Ryan said, taking me by the hand.

I smiled even wider. "And, well, you're gay and all," I joked.

Ryan laughed. "I am *so* not."

210

Then he pulled me into his arms and kissed me. I kissed him back, even through my laughter. He picked me up with one arm wrapped around me and carried me into his room, slamming the door behind us with his foot.

eleven

It's your senior prom. He likes you. And if he likes you that much, he'll want to go with you.

I glanced at the address on the scrap of paper in my hand and looked up at the old colonial house in front of me. It was Friday night, and I was supposed to be meeting Ryan and his friends at Brody Walsh's off-campus house so we could all go to a concert together. One of Lazy Daze's favorite bands was coming to play, and half his school had bought tickets. Ryan, thoughtful as ever, scored an extra one for me.

And after a week of sweet phone calls that lasted way into the night, I had decided it was time for me to pop the question. Now. In person. When he saw how much it meant to me, he'd have to cave and say he'd be my date. He'd just have to.

Otherwise there was a decent possibility I'd be staying home on prom night. That was *so* not an option.

I rolled my shoulders back and walked up the three steps to the door. Inside, I could hear a ton of shouting and laughter, and the music was turned up to a deafening level. Knocking seemed rather pointless, so I held my breath and opened the door.

The first thing I saw was Johnny Jackman, the guitarist, running past me as he sprayed champagne everywhere. He laughed with his head thrown back, chasing one of the groupie girls from the concert, who shrieked at the top of her lungs. In the background tons of people chatted and cheered and handed out bottles of beer. Clearly, there was a celebration going on.

"Noelle!"

Ryan rushed over from a crowd of people near the fireplace, lifted me up in his arms, and twirled me around.

"Hey! Nice to see you, too!" I shouted.

"We did it! We made the finals!" Ryan told me gleefully. He set me down on the floor and gave me a celebratory kiss. "We're going to the Showdown!" he cheered, loudly enough to make the tendons in his neck pop out. Everyone else in the house responded with hollers of joy.

"I knew it!" I shouted, hugging him again. "I *knew* you'd make it!"

Ryan held me so tightly, I could barely breathe. "You have to come," he said into my ear. "You have to be there. My good-luck charm."

I leaned back and looked him in the eye. "Are you

kidding? Of course I'll be there!"

He kissed me again, and I knew for sure I was stressing about nothing when it came to the prom. Look how much I meant to him. There was no way he was going to turn me down. Not when he realized how important it was to me.

"Dude! Check out the flyers Lea made up!" Brody said, rushing over to us, all hyper. "The girl is mad talented."

He handed over a white flyer, and Ryan and I both checked it out. At the top was the circular Lazy Daze logo, drawn by hand, and underneath was all the info for the Showdown.

"We're gonna put these up all over campus tomorrow," Brody said. "At the Showdown the bouncer's gonna ask everyone as they come in which band they're there to see. Those record company guys are gonna know everyone turned out to see Lazy Daze!"

"Whoo-hoo!" Johnny shouted from across the room, dousing himself in champagne.

"Here. Take one," Ryan said, handing the flyer to me. "Maybe you can get some people from your school to come."

"Totally," I replied with a smile.

"Want something to drink?" he asked me.

"I'll take a soda," I said.

Ryan squeezed my hand and hurried off toward the kitchen. I glanced at the flyer again. This was insane. They actually had a shot at a recording contract. In a few weeks Ryan could be making an album.

I had to get all my friends to come. They would *love* it. I whipped out my phone and was about to call Aurora to give her the info, when my eyes fell on the Showdown date.

The entire world came screeching to a halt.

June eighth. June *eighth*?

I swallowed hard, feeling sick to my stomach. Apparently I wouldn't be getting a bunch of people from my school to show up. At least not seniors.

The Showdown was the exact same night as the senior prom.

Saturday afternoon, I took out my prom dress and hung it up on my closet door. Then I pulled out my prom tickets and sat down in my desk chair. I fingered the gold filigree border on the thick white cards and stared at the pretty pink beading on the bodice of my dress.

I could give this stuff up, couldn't I? I didn't really *need* to go to the prom. I mean, so what if I'd been dreaming about it basically my entire life? This was Ryan's future we were talking about here!

So why did my whole body feel sick at the thought?

"This totally sucks," I said under my breath.

"You talking to yourself again?" my sister asked, sticking her head into my room.

My hands flew to my chest. "Scare the crap out of me, why don't you?"

Faith pushed open the door and walked into my room. "What's the matter? Why are you staring at your prom dress as if it holds the meaning of life?"

She crossed her arms over her chest and raised one eyebrow behind her square glasses. Suddenly I remembered there were benefits to having an older sister. Right here in my very room was someone who had, very recently, been through all this stuff.

"Faith, do you think you'd regret it if you had missed your senior prom?" I asked, tossing the tickets onto my desk.

"That snoozefest? Are you kidding?" she said. She plopped down onto my bed. "I would've been better off staying home to watch that Buffy marathon."

I laughed. "There was a Buffy marathon on that night?"

"Yes! And the fact that I remember just goes to show how very lame the night was for me," she said. "But you? I don't know."

"What do you mean?" I asked, even though I had a feeling I knew what she was going to say.

"Noelle, I was never that big on all that high school crap," she said. "You know, sports and spirit and 'Omigod! We're going to keep in touch for the rest of our lives!'" she said dramatically, clasping her hands together. "But you? You live for that stuff."

"Thanks," I said sarcastically.

"It's not a bad thing! We're just different," she told me. "I wouldn't regret missing the prom. You, however, probably would. You'd probably stay up nights sobbing about it until you get old and you're all wrinkled and smelly."

"Great." I slumped slightly and stared. Not exactly the pep talk I'd been looking for.

"What's going on? Do you have another offer for that night or something?" she asked.

"Yeah. Ryan's band is playing in this Showdown thing in the city and—"

"The Showdown!? You have got to be kidding me," Faith said, standing up. "His band made it to the Showdown?"

"You know about it?" I asked, surprised.

"Everyone knows about it! That's a huge deal!" Faith exclaimed. "And he wants you to go?"

"Uh, yeah."

"Then you *have* to go. Noelle, the Showdown is, like, *impossible* to get into," she said. "And your boyfriend would be in one of the bands? That is *so* cool!"

"What happened to 'You'll regret missing your prom until you smell'?" I asked.

"Screw the prom! Screw high school! This is real life! It's the city! It's hot boys in bands!" she cried, curling her fingers into fists.

"I literally don't think I've ever seen you this excited," I told her with a laugh.

"Then take me seriously!" Faith said. "You have to go to this. It'll be so much cooler than some alcohol-free, twinkle-light, and chicken Kiev crapfest."

I laughed, suddenly feeling much happier. "You're right," I said. "Screw high school! It's practically over anyway. Who needs it?"

I grabbed the prom tickets off my desk and was about to tear them in half, when something stopped me. I stared down at the swirly script, the words *Jefferson High School Senior Prom*, and I just couldn't do it. Instead I whipped open my desk drawer, shoved them inside, and slammed it shut.

"Way to make a statement, Noelle," Faith said dryly.

"One step at a time," I told her.

I could feel Ryan watching me as I raced forward to return a short lob to my opponent, Genevieve Price, and I smiled. Even in the heat of battle, just knowing Ryan was there made me smile.

Genevieve returned my shot, and I reached for it, turning my racket to slam it directly into the court six inches from the net. She had backed up in anticipation of a long shot, and she had no chance. She dove for it but missed by a mile.

"Game! Set! Match! Bairstow!"

The crowd cheered, but no one louder than Ryan. As I shook Genevieve's hand, he stuffed his fingers into his mouth and whistled. It was so piercing, a few people winced.

"Nice win!" Ryan said as he loped down the metal bleachers in his black boots. "You went all Sharapova on that girl!"

I laughed and shoved my racket into its bag. "What does that mean?"

Ryan blanched slightly. "Isn't that how you pronounce it? I thought she was some sick tennis player."

"Oh, no. She is," I said. "I just thought you meant I did something specific that was, you know, Sharapova-esque."

Ryan reached for my duffel bag and slung it over his

shoulder without even asking. "Actually, I wouldn't know. I didn't get that far in my research."

I paused. "You did research? Again?"

"Not did. Am doing," he said, walking backward as we headed for the parking lot. "It's an ongoing thing."

"That's so—"

"What?" Ryan asked.

"I don't know. Totally unnecessary and yet ridiculously sweet?" I suggested.

Ryan tilted his head and turned to walk next to me. "I just wanted to find out more about the sport, you know, since it's such a big part of your life."

I felt warm all over and not from the sun. Ryan cared about me. *Really* cared. Like took time out of his busy college-student/drummer/barista life to read up on things that were important to me.

I gazed at his profile, and I knew. This was a person I was willing to miss the prom for. There were just certain things way more important than a high school dance.

"So, what else have you learned?" I asked.

"Well, I read a lot about the Williams sisters. I even watched one of their old matches on ESPN Classics. Which, by the way, was a channel I didn't even know I had," he said. "Those girls throw more aces than anyone."

I laughed. "You don't throw an ace."

"Oh. Sorry. They've aced more people—"

"Actually, an *ace* is really more of a noun, not a verb," I said.

Ryan's brow knit. "This sport is more complicated than

I thought," he deadpanned.

I looped an arm through his and kept walking. "Don't worry. I'm sure that together, we can figure it all out."

"It is going to kick *ass*," Jonah proclaimed as he approached our lunch table on Monday afternoon. "My dad is going all out, dude. It'll be even *better* than the prom."

I squirmed slightly as he sat down and I saw that he'd been talking to Zach, who was trailing behind him. Zach glanced at me coolly, then sat down at the far end of the table. He hadn't joined us since our breakup, and I was surprised to see him here now, considering he hadn't deigned to talk to me since I'd told him we weren't getting back together.

"What're you guys talking about?" Aurora asked, popping a baby carrot into her mouth.

"Jonah's post-prom party," Danielle told us, sliding into the seat across from mine. She grabbed her lemonade and shook it up. "His dad is renting out one of those party boats that cruises the lake. Jonah's inviting half the class."

"The cool half," Jonah said with a laugh, then slapped hands with Zach.

"Sweet. Drake and I will definitely be there," Aurora said. She glanced at Zach, then looked at me mischievously. I could feel the drama coming on. "So, Noelle, have you asked *Ryan* yet?"

Zach looked up. His face turned red. I could have killed Aurora. But then, what was I supposed to do? Protect Zach from the details of my social life forever? He was going to find out sooner or later.

"Actually, no," I told her, clearing my throat. I looked around at my friends, feeling almost sorry for them. They were going to flip out when they heard what was coming next. "I don't think I'm going to the prom."

"What?" every single one of them exclaimed in unison. Including Zach.

"Well. Hello there," I said to him, trying to deflect a little of the attention.

"I'm sorry, but you've gotta be kidding," he protested. "Suzy High School not going to her own senior prom?"

"No, it's just that Ryan's band made it into this huge competition thing in Chicago that night, and they might even get signed by a record label. I can't ask him to miss that."

"So go with someone else," Zach said.

"I . . . can't."

"Why? Are you, like, seeing this guy now? I thought he was gay."

"He's not," I told him, swallowing hard. "I just recently found out that he's not," I clarified, hoping to put the subject to rest.

"Lucky girl," Danielle said under her breath, winking at me.

"What?" Jonah asked.

"Nothing!" she trilled, smiling sweetly. She rubbed his upper arm and smooched his cheek. "I love you!"

Jonah smiled and went back to his lunch.

"Anyway, it looks like I'll be going to this Showdown thing that night," I said, shrugging. Trying to make it look as if I was totally and completely fine with the whole situation.

"I'm sorry, but I cannot approve of this plan," Danielle stated, scrunching up a napkin and tossing it onto her tray. "I don't care how hot the guy is. I can't imagine the prom without you."

"This band of his better be the next Coldplay," Aurora muttered.

"They are, you guys. Well, not Coldplay exactly, but they're *so* good," I gushed.

"I'd have to see for myself," Danielle said. "Then *maybe* I'll be able to give my stamp of approval."

"Then why don't you?" I suggested. "They have a gig on campus this weekend. We could all go!"

Aurora and Danielle looked at Jonah and Zach.

"I'm sorry, I just don't believe this," Zach said, glaring directly at me. "I don't believe that you, of all people, are going to miss the senior prom. You've been looking forward to it for three years."

My stomach clenched as I stared back at him. *"No, Zach,"* I wanted to say. *"We've been looking forward to it for three years. But you kind of screwed all that up when you went for Melanie Faison."*

"Well, things change," I said finally.

"Not this much." Zach shook his head. "I just don't think you should let this guy make you miss the prom, that's all."

Oddly, I actually felt touched at this sentiment. Maybe Zach did still care about me, at least a little. And he knew me well. Part of me couldn't believe I was missing the prom either. But at least I knew it was for a good reason.

"He's not *making* me do anything," I said. "This was my decision. So, who wants to go see Lazy Daze this weekend?" I added quickly, dying for a subject change.

"I've got better things to do, thanks," Zach said grumpily.

"I'll be doing better things with him," Jonah said.

"Fine. Be lame," Danielle told them. "We're in, right, Aurora?"

"I've been looking for an excuse to wear my new purple leather pants," she said with a shrug.

"Cool," I said, shaking off the negativity Zach had brought down on me. "This is going to be fun."

twelve

"Noelle, did you sell your soul to the devil or something?" Aurora asked as Lazy Daze launched into their last song. "He is *so* lickable."

I laughed as I watched Ryan get into the beat. "By me. Lickable by me," I said.

"Of course. I would never lick another friend's man," Aurora said, taking a sip of her soda. "That lead singer, however . . . "

"He's taken," I told her.

"Oh yeah? By whom?" Danielle asked, jumping into the conversation.

"By Marie." I pointed across the auditorium at Brody's girlfriend. She was dancing with Lea and Jeannie, looking ultra gorgeous in a red halter top and jeans.

Aurora's face fell. "Damn."

"Well, whatever," Danielle said. "The point is, you are *so* excused from the prom, Noelle. Ryan is delish. As if we didn't already know that."

"Yeah. And this band? They're going places," Aurora said with a nod. Brody launched into a perfect, long wail, squeezing his eyes closed as everyone around us cheered. "Are you *sure* he's taken?"

"Positive." I laughed. "And thank you for the free pass."

We turned and made our way through the bopping crowd toward the back of the room. Several guys checked out Aurora's tight purple pants, and by the time we got to the wall, she was smiling again. Forget Brody. She could pretty much have any other guy in the place.

"I kind of like it here," Aurora said, looking around.

"Me, too. It's so weird. A few weeks ago I'd never set foot on this campus, and now I feel like I kind of belong here."

"Thinking about bagging Princeton and coming here?" Danielle teased.

"Hardly," I said. "It's just nice. Don't you feel older just being here?"

"Yeah. There's this, like, freedom," Danielle said as a couple of girls danced by. "I can't wait to get out of high school."

I sighed as I leaned against a cinder-block wall, covered with posters advertising various clubs and events.

"I can't believe I'm actually skipping the senior prom."

"I know. It's gonna be so weird," Danielle said, leaning

next to me. "But, hey! Maybe you could still make the after-party!"

"Yeah! It's gonna be sick!" Aurora agreed, her eyes lighting up. "Way sicker than the prom."

A flicker of hope sparked in my chest, and I pushed myself up straight. "That's not a bad idea," I said as Ryan finished up the set with a crash of cymbals. The whole place erupted with cheers and applause. "I mean, if it's gonna be *way* sicker," I teased, shouting to be heard over the noise.

"It's the perfect compromise!" Danielle told me. "You do his thing, then come do your thing."

I nodded anxiously. "If the timing works out," I said.

"The prom's not even over 'til eleven," Aurora pointed out. "And the boat doesn't leave 'til twelve. How many songs do these guys hafta do? I mean, seriously, all they need to do is walk out onstage and they'd get my vote."

Over Danielle's shoulder, I saw Ryan weaving his way through the crowd. "Shh. We'll talk about this later," I told them.

I hadn't even mentioned the prom to Ryan yet. There was no way I wanted him to feel any guilt about my missing it.

"Hey," Ryan said, wrapping me up in his semi-sweaty arms. "Thanks for coming."

"Of course. My friends were dying to see the band," I replied, my heart pumping away just from being near him. "You remember Danielle and Aurora."

"How could I forget?" Ryan said, nodding at them.

"We *are* pretty unforgettable," Aurora said, slipping an arm through Ryan's. "Now, let's talk about this Brody guy. How serious *is* he about longhair girl? Cuz I can get extensions if that's what it takes."

Ryan shot me a half-amused, half-concerned look over one shoulder as Aurora led him away. Danielle and I laughed and waved. If Ryan was going to be with me, he'd have to get used to Aurora. The sooner, the better.

On the night of the senior prom and the Showdown, I parked my car in front of Danielle's house and looked down at my outfit, handpicked by Faith. Old jeans, layered black and army-green tank tops, long beaded necklace, killer platform sandals. Not exactly what I had been expecting to wear on prom night. But then, nothing about this night was expected.

I checked my watch as another car pulled up behind mine. Luke, in full tuxedo, stepped out of the backseat and opened the door for Lena, dressed to kill in a red gown. Luke's parents jumped out of the front seat and instantly started snapping pictures like a couple of caffeine-tweaked paparazzi. I laughed to myself wistfully. Ah, prom night.

With a deep breath I got out of the car and walked behind Luke and his family to the backyard. All my friends were gathered around in gorgeous dresses, their hair curled and pinned and sprayed. A few tiaras twinkled in the late-afternoon sun, and skirts swished everywhere. The guys looked red-carpet ready in their tuxes, their hair all slicked and their cheeks freshly shaved. Parents hovered, cooing over the dresses and wielding video cameras. Suddenly I wondered what I was doing here.

"Noelle! You came!" Danielle screeched.

She and Aurora raced toward me, all satin and perfume, and I was caught up in a four-armed hug. I closed my eyes and hugged them back.

Right. *This* was what I was doing here.

"You look hot," Danielle said, pulling back.

"Please! Me? Hello, Miss Cleavage!" I said, checking out her dress.

"If you got it, flaunt it," Danielle replied. "I just wish I could hold this thing up."

She grabbed either side of her black strapless dress and yanked it neckward in a very unladylike fashion.

"Noelle, *mija*, you're here! Thank goodness!" Danielle's mother cried, bustling over with her camera. "It wouldn't be prom night if I couldn't get a picture of the three of you together."

"Thanks, Mrs. Ruiz," I said.

Okay, here came the tears. I was not going to get all weepy and nostalgic. I was not. But when I glanced at Aurora, her black eyeliner was already starting to run.

"Do not cry! This is not a big deal!" I told her.

"I know. And you are going to have *soooo* much fun tonight," she whispered, her voice cracking.

"You are. You are, you are," Danielle added, managing to maintain dry eyes.

"Okay! Get together and smile!" Mrs. Ruiz called.

Danielle and Aurora gathered in on either side of me and squeezed. Hard. Like they were never letting go.

"They are *so* gonna win this thing!" Marie shouted gleefully as we jumped up and down in front of the stage.

"Look at all these people! They're loving it!" I shouted back.

All around us people were dancing and moshing to Lazy Daze. It was impossible not to. When we first arrived, I had been all nervous butterflies on Ryan's behalf, especially when I saw the size of the place. The Showdown was in a larger venue than the preliminary round, and everything looked huge—from the lights to the stage to the audience. But my nerves had long since settled. The guys had completely taken over the monster stage, running around and jamming with one another. Brody had even jumped up on top of the speakers during the first song, which had sent everyone into a frenzy. Luckily, the entire audience area was wide open, with no seating to speak of, making it easier for the fans to turn it into a dance floor.

Dance floor. I glanced at my watch and wondered what Danielle and Aurora were doing at the prom. Were they dancing? Eating? Had the king and queen been named yet?

"Got someplace better to be?" Marie teased.

I shoved my watch arm behind me. "Not at all!"

"Good! Because we're going up there!" she shouted.

"Up where?"

My heart dropped when I looked up and saw that Brody was pointing his finger at us, then crooking it toward him.

"Up *there!*"

"It's the finale song!" Lea shouted, grabbing my arm as she twirled by. "'Dance, Girls, Dance!' We always go up for this one!"

"What? Since when?" I cried, my heart slamming around as they yanked me toward the stage stairs. Already Jeannie and a few of the other regular groupies were climbing up there.

Before I knew it, a bunch of girls were dancing around onstage with Johnny, Brody, and Crash, the bassist. Marie strode over to Brody and ground him with her hips from behind, totally sexy and totally sure of herself. Brody just kept right on singing, loving every minute of it.

"Come on!" Lea shouted, taking me by the hand.

She twirled me into the center of the stage, and I looked at Ryan. He grinned and egged me on, shouting over the deafening music. There was nothing I could do. Nothing but dance, girl, dance.

And so I did. I held on to Lea's hand, and we twirled each other around and totally got down. I couldn't help thinking of Aurora and Danielle and wishing they were there to do this with me. Or that I could be at the prom dancing with them. But one more look at Ryan, and I remembered why I was here. Soon enough I started laughing and running around, dancing with the other girls. I didn't even care what I looked like; I was just having fun.

Meanwhile, the crowd was going absolutely nuts. Brody got up front and sang the last few bars of the raucous song, and we all joined him, shouting at the top of our lungs. By the time Ryan finished it off with a crash of drums, everyone was out of breath, sweating, and completely high on life. The crowd screamed and shouted and jumped up and down as the MC fought his way to the front of the stage.

"That was Lazy Daze, everybody!" he shouted into his microphone. "Let's give them and their *ladies* a big round of applause!"

He didn't even need to ask. The place was already out of control. Suddenly someone grabbed me around my waist from behind and lifted me up. I screamed and turned around to hug Ryan.

"That was incredible!" I shouted.

"You're incredible!" he shouted back.

And then he kissed me as the crowd began to chant. "Lazy Daze! Lazy Daze!"

I could feel Ryan's heart pounding against my chest, and I smiled. This was way better than any senior prom. As if I'd ever needed to make a choice.

Every instant Ryan took his eyes off me, I found myself staring at my watch. Time was ticking by faster than it ever had before. Seriously. Why couldn't time pass this quickly when I was in calculus class?

Fifteen minutes more and it would be too late to make it to the after-party. On the other hand, why was I even still contemplating it? I had never even told Ryan what was going on. Did I really think I was going to get him out of here and to the dock before the boat took off?

Wake up and smell the reality, Noelle. Prom night is officially over.

"Oh, my God. Here we go," Ryan said suddenly, slipping his hand into mine. The MC was taking the stage. He had a card in his hand. A card that held the name of the winner.

Instantly my heart hit my throat. The entire band and their entourage were gathered on the floor near the right side of the stage. Seconds ago everyone had been nervously chatting and laughing and drinking. Now the room was riveted.

"Please, please, please," I heard Brody whispering over and over again. Marie rubbed his arm and gave it a squeeze.

I looked up at Ryan and wondered what he was thinking.

"All right, everyone, it's about that time!" the MC said, earning a few whoops from the crowd. "It was a tough decision. We had five kick-ass bands this year."

A roar of approval went up all around us, and I smiled. Ryan bounced up and down on the balls of his feet. I could relate. He just wanted to get this over with. It was like waiting for a final serve in a match.

"But only one kick-ass band can win," the MC continued. "And that kick-ass band, the winner of representation with the Garret Group and a record contract with MAC Records is . . . "

"Please, please, *PLEASE!*"

"Lazy Daze!"

The entire club erupted with the force of ten volcanoes. Ryan whipped me up into his arms and hugged the air right out of me. All around us his bandmates and their friends were screaming and cheering.

"Congratulations!" I shouted, laughing.

"Thank you! Thank you! Thank you!" he cried.

From the corner of my eye I saw Brody, Johnny, and Crash rushing the stage.

"Uh, you'd better go," I said, tapping his shoulder.

Ryan set me down, looked me in the eye, and then kissed me, long and firm and soft all at once. By the time he finally let me go, I could barely stand. He grinned his heart-flipping grin, then turned and ran up to join his band.

"Whoa," I said, nearly swooning.

"That was some kiss," Marie told me, knocking me with one elbow.

"Tell me about it."

We all watched as the band accepted their trophy—two golden guns pointing from opposite directions at a record—and posed for pictures with the record company people. I couldn't have stopped grinning if I'd tried. But then, I also found myself checking my watch again. It was like a reflex. Really had to get control of that.

Ryan shook hands and posed . . . and posed and shook hands . . . while time *tick, tick, tick*ed away. Finally it seemed definitely too late to make the after-party. I found myself a seat on one of the benches near a wall and took a deep breath.

It was okay. It was. There would be plenty of parties all summer. It wasn't as if I was never going to see my friends again.

"Hey."

I looked up to find Ryan hovering over me. He looked concerned. I was snagged. I quickly plastered a smile onto my face. "Hey there, rock star!"

"What's wrong?" he asked.

"Nothing! I'm fine!" I said, standing. I shoved my hands into the back pockets of my jeans and tried to look non-chalant.

"Uh, yeah, right," Ryan said. "I've seen that look before. What's wrong?"

"Nothing! It's just . . . "

Ryan took my hand and ducked so that he could see into my eyes. "What?"

All around us people were backslapping and chugging beers. I felt totally conspicuous having this serious moment.

"It's just my prom," I said finally, feeling like a heel. Where was my self-control?

"What about your prom?" Ryan asked, his brow knitting.

"It's kind of . . . happening right now," I said.

Ryan took a step back. "*What!?*"

"Yeah . . . "

"Noelle! Why didn't you *tell* me!?" he said.

"Because! What were you going to do? Miss *this*!?" I

235

replied, throwing my hands up. "This is the biggest night of your life!"

"So? This is your senior prom! I know what that means to you!" he said. He seemed almost angry. "You could have at least told me."

"Why? So you could feel guilty?" I asked. "I didn't want it to become a whole your-thing-or-my-thing *thing*."

"Noelle, at least if you had told me about it, we might have been able to figure something out," he said. "I feel awful."

Damn. Here I was, trying to make sure I didn't screw everything up, and I had achieved the exact opposite.

"I'm sorry," I said.

"No. *I'm* sorry," he replied. "From now on you have to tell me stuff like this. I want to know what's going on with you."

I smiled slightly, touched. "Okay."

"So, is it really too late? Can we make any of it?" he asked.

I scoffed a laugh, even though this was what I'd been hoping for all night long. Now I realized how totally impossible it would be. "Please. Don't you want to party with your friends? You just won a freakin' record contract!"

"Yeah. And we'll still have it in the morning," he told me. "Do you want to go?"

"Ryan—"

"We've done enough of my stuff tonight," he said firmly. "It's your turn."

He rendered me breathless.

"Well, there *is* this after-party thing," I said tentatively.

"Good," Ryan said, grabbing me by the hand. "Let's go."

"What!?" I asked with a laugh. "You can't be serious! I'm not even sure we can make it! It's kind of on a boat."

"We'll make it," he said, dragging me across the club.

"Dude! Where're you going!?" Brody shouted as we passed him and Marie. "We're going on a bar crawl!"

"Not me!" Ryan shouted back. "*I* am going to a prom."

"There it is!" I shouted, pointing out the window as Ryan swung his car into a spot and slammed on the brakes.

The party boat couldn't have been more obvious. The outside was strung with hundreds of red paper lanterns, and there was a huge banner on the side that read SENIORS RULE! Lame but very easy to spot.

"We made it!" Ryan cried.

There was a toot of a horn, and my stomach dropped. The boat was about to take off. Ryan jumped out of the car.

"We'll have to run!" he shouted.

I raced around the car and grabbed his hand. Together we ran through the parking lot, sprinting like mad over dirt and gravel. The closer we got, I was able to make out some people along the decks. Girls in colorful dresses, guys in their tuxes with their ties undone. Everyone was laughing and having a good time. I had to make this boat. I just had to.

"Wait!" I shouted. "Hold the boat!"

A couple of people noticed us, and everyone turned to watch. Suddenly Aurora, Danielle, and Jonah pushed through the crowd at the back of the boat. Jonah took one look at us and turned around again, hopefully going to stop the captain.

"Noelle! Come on!" Danielle shouted, waving us on. "Come on! You can make it!"

"Run! Run for your life!" Aurora cried.

Ryan and I glanced at each other and really turned it on. Our feet hit the boards of the dock, and the whole thing shook as we barreled our way toward the gangplank.

"Go! Go! Go!" a few people cheered, watching us.

"Stop the boat!" Aurora shouted.

We were fifteen feet away. Ten. The gangplank started to lift, its mechanism wailing as it cranked away.

"Oh, crap," Ryan said.

"Don't stop!" I shouted.

"Seriously?" he said with a squeak.

"We can make it!" I cried back.

I was not going to come this close, only to turn back now. This was my senior prom. I already had the perfect date, and he'd already had his perfect night. Now it was my turn.

"Do it! Do it!" a few kids cried from above.

We got to the end of the dock and leaped into the air, hands clutched. I let out a shriek of triumph as my feet came down on the gangplank, stumbled slightly, and then righted myself. Everyone cheered.

"Yes!" I shouted.

Ryan

Ryan grabbed me, his chest heaving, and kissed me as my classmates slapped us on our backs. Who needed the prom and the big fluffy dress? This was already the best night of my life.

The End

The Choice Redux

Don't you love a happy ending? Yeah, so do I. But if you're somehow unsatisfied with this one, well, then, I can't stop you from turning back to page 99 and trying again. But don't say I didn't warn you.

Here's a sneak peek at

Hook Up or Break Up #4

Don't Do Anything I Wouldn't Do

I screwed up my courage, rolled my shoulders back, and picked my way along the cracked front walk to Nicholas's house. It was a low stucco structure with at least ten random beach chairs strewn across the lawn, along with a cooler, a couple dozen crushed beer cans, a folded-up beach umbrella, and several pairs of muddy sneakers. The porch light flickered and I could hear music coming from one of the upstairs windows, which was half-draped over by a striped sheet.

I tried the doorbell, but heard nothing so I knocked. Then I knocked again. My face started to heat up. I felt like someone *had* to be watching me and laughing at me. My first inclination was to turn around and flee, but then I remembered this summer was all about going against instinct.

I held my breath, lifted my fist, and pounded.

Nicholas opened the door two seconds later. My breath caught in my chest. I was pretty sure that he was getting better looking every time I saw him. His tan seemed deeper somehow, and he wore a blue button-down shirt open at the neck, with the sleeves casually rolled. There were those forearms again. Sigh.

"Jenna! Hi!" he said with that easy grin.

I completely relaxed even as my guts totally turned to mush. "Hi."

"Great! You brought the food. I haven't eaten since breakfast." He took the bags from me and stepped aside so I could walk in. Then he kicked the door closed. The living room had a kind of stale smell and all the furniture was mismatched and haphazardly placed. On the wall above an old stone fireplace was a huge Corona mirror with a crack through the center. There were fast-food bags and old six-pack cartons shoved into a pile in the corner and a cat sat on one of the chairs, lazily licking himself. It was actually kind of . . . gross.

"I'm so sorry about the mess. I swear I don't normally live like this," Nicholas said. "We have these summer sublets and they really just let the place go to hell. I'm hardly ever here so I don't notice it until someone comes over and I see their face."

I flushed. "Sorry. Was I making a face?"

Nicholas grinned. "It's perfectly natural, considering.

That's why I suggested we eat outside."

"Lead the way," I said with a smile.

Together we walked through a simple, dimly lit kitchen and out a sliding door onto the patio. Now this was more like it. A small glass-topped table had been set with red plastic plates and cups. Votive candles flickered, making a centerpiece, and a few more candles were set atop an outdoor bar and along a bench near the wall. I could hear the surf crashing into the shore somewhere behind the hedge that surrounded the yard, and a small stereo on the bar played jazz music.

"This is nice," I said.

"Thanks. Have a seat."

I did, and Nicholas placed the bags on the table and started removing boxes and trays. He shoved the empty bag into a garbage can, handed me some chopsticks, and sat down. As he started heaping food onto his plate, I stared at the chopsticks. There was no other available silverware.

"Uh . . . do you have a fork I could use?" I asked.

Nicholas blinked. "Come on. You can't eat Chinese food with a fork." He broke his chopsticks apart, deftly picked up a piece of Tso's chicken, and popped it in his mouth. "It's easy. Here. Hold 'em like this."

He held up his hand. I already knew this was not going to go well. It wasn't as if I had never tried to use chopsticks before. The experiments just always ended with me shooting shrimp across the room or dropping sweet-and-sour sauce right into my lap. Still, I didn't want him to think I was unwilling, so I broke the sticks apart and tried to mimic his grip.

"Good," he said. "Now you just lift."

There was no food on my plate yet, so I tipped the box of beef and broccoli toward my dish and coaxed out a few spears. I tried to lift one of the larger pieces of green, but it slid right off and plopped back onto the plate.

"You're trying too hard," Nicholas said. Half his food was already gone. "Here."

He placed his hand around mine and adjusted the sticks, then held on to my fingers as we went for a piece of beef together. For a split second I gripped the tiny morsel, but then the chopsticks came together and the beef splattered on the table.

"Damn," I said under my breath. There was no way I could sit here and humiliate myself like this all night. I was just going to get redder and redder until Nicholas realized what an unworldly, whiny baby I was. How I wished for a fork.

"It's okay. I have a solution," Nicholas said.

A fork?

"I'll just have to feed you."

He picked up a piece of broccoli with his chopsticks and slid closer to me. I looked at him dubiously.

"You're serious."

"I never joke about food," he said. "Do you want to eat or not?"

I laughed and opened my mouth, hoping I didn't look like one of those wide-mouthed bass my dad was always tossing into the boat on fishing trips. But Nicholas didn't recoil in horror. Instead he placed the broccoli gently on my tongue and the flavors filled my senses. Ah. Finally.

Food. I chewed and swallowed and he was ready with the next piece.

"I feel kind of silly," I said, opening my mouth again.

"Don't," he replied.

He fed me a piece of the beef, then some rice. With each mouthful, he inched a bit closer to me, until his knee was between my legs. Finally, I swallowed a bit of food and realized I was looking directly into his eyes.

"More?" he asked.

I shook my head slowly. The candles flickered in a soft breeze. "I'm good."

"Good," he said. Then he grabbed my face in his hands and kissed me.

Hook Up or Break Up

One girl. Three guys. You decide.

Hook Up or Break Up #1: Love Is Random Too

Quinn Donohue is the ultimate tomboy. She loves skateboarding—and Josh Marx. But when she sees him making out with another girl, her best friend decides it's time for drastic measures, and she makes Quinn choose three guys at random and ask each one out. Owen (the strong, silent type), Corey (who's practically her best friend), and Max (the hotter than hot exchange student from Australia) all say yes. You decide which one Quinn hooks up with in the end!

Hook Up or Break Up #2: If You Can't Be Good, Be Good at It

Layla has a "fast" reputation due to her lively personality and incredible good looks—and the fact that she just REALLY likes boys. But it's senior year and she's finally settled down with Nate, a gorgeous jock. Still, she can't help but notice Ian, with his funky dreads and dreamy British accent. And then Drew, the hot, rebellious artist she's had a crush on since she was 15, crashes into her life. Just when things couldn't be more confusing, Layla makes two too many plans for Valentine's Day. You decide which boy Layla hooks up with in the end!

HARPER TEEN
An Imprint of HarperCollins Publishers

www.harperteen.com

PARACHUTE PRESS